"Ki, this . . . this Death Angel. Is he good?"

"Very good. Also cold and without mercy."

"I haven't heard of him before," Jessie said.

"The Death Angel is said to be a man with almost supernatural talent, one who has absorbed all the skills of *jujutsu, atemi, kenjutsu*—but he uses them only to kill."

"Isn't it odd that he should be connected with this business? What would the cartel have in mind, to send him here?"

Ki turned slowly and looked at Jessie. "The cartel knows we are here, and it knows why. The Death Angel has been sent to kill me . . ."

WESLEY ELLIS

LONE STAR
AND THE
AMARILLO RIFLES

A JOVE BOOK

LONE STAR AND THE AMARILLO RIFLES

A Jove book / published by arrangement with
the author

PRINTING HISTORY
Jove edition / January 1985

ISBN: 0-515-08082-9

Jove books are published by The Berkley Publishing Group,
200 Madison Avenue, New York, N.Y. 10016. The words
"A JOVE BOOK" and the "J" with sunburst are trademarks
belonging to Jove Publications, Inc.

PRINTED IN THE UNITED STATES OF AMERICA

Chapter 1

He was tall, his face as craggy and scarred as the red mesa country surrounding Cheney's hideout. His eyes were as black as obsidian, as cold and unfeeling as a rattler's. His name was Chato Cruz, and every law enforcement man and army unit on either side of the border for five hundred miles was looking for him.

Ray Cheney stood in the doorway of the dilapidated log cabin, watching Cruz. Down the canyon, camped among the cedars, were fifty men Cruz could count as loyal to him. There would be more later. It takes an army to make revolution, and that was what Cheney had in mind.

"Hot son of a bitch," Cruz growled in his accented English. It was just a manner of greeting people. Cruz was untouched by heat, by cold, by fear. Just now his face was dry, cool, and relaxed. "Any word from these big friends of yours?"

Ray Cheney, who was slight, blond, and redfaced, didn't like the sarcastic emphasis Cruz gave the words "big friends," but that was all right. His friends were big enough, all right. Big enough to show Cruz where the door to hell was, when the time came. Just now they needed the *bandido*.

"I got a letter this morning," Cheney said, leading the way into the stuffy, filthy cabin where Cheney and six men had been holing up for three long months.

"Yes?" Cruz looked around, removed his hat, and found the tequila bottle Cheney had been sucking at. Cruz took a deep swig, swirled the liquor around in the bottle, then took another.

"The arms are on their way. They'll be leaving Amarillo on the fourteenth."

"Bueno," Cruz said. He slapped the bottle down on the table, and Cheney jumped. The Mexican smiled. It wasn't a very pretty expression. Cruz despised weakness. He had never found any occasion when it was of the slightest use. Cruz even liked his women hard. Because he was harder, and if they wanted to make a game of it, fine.

"You'd better start calling the rest of your men over," Cheney suggested. Cruz nodded without looking at the American. Cheney wasn't going to tell him what to do, ever. He didn't like Cheney, but he was willing to work with him for now. The stakes were very high, but Chato Cruz believed he had all the cards. Cheney's "big friends"— if they existed—were far away. Over the ocean. They were sending money, arms, and advice. The advice could always be ignored.

Cruz swaggered out, taking the bottle with him, and Ray Cheney stood in the sunlit doorway of the cabin, staring after the dark outaw.

You'll get yours, Cheney silently promised Cruz's back. He waited until Cruz had swung aboard his blue roan and ridden off, tiny puffs of cinnamon-colored dust marking his trail; then, with a violent curse, Cheney went back in, found a fresh bottle of liquor, and sat down to do some serious brooding.

The Amarillo stationmaster peered out the window of the colorless depot building. He couldn't see the 4:30 yet, but then the railroad's schedule was something of a joke. Optimistic, but not exactly informative. It was hot. Hot outside, hot inside the squat little station building. It didn't seem to bother the man who stood out on the platform waiting for the 4:30.

He looked cool and very calm, as if there were nothing in the world but time, and nothing to do but use it.

He might have been an Indian, but the stationmaster didn't think he was. He might have been some kind of Chinaman, but he was too tall for that. Far too tall. He wasn't a bad looking man, dark and erect. He was lean, but he moved with a kind of gracefulness that bespoke quiet confidence in his own strength and abilities. He wore black jeans, a white collarless shirt, a scuffed black leather vest. On his head was a low-crowned, wide-brimmed hat that shaded dark, scrutinizing eyes.

There was something about the man . . . but then the stationmaster heard the distant whistle and gave up worrying about the stranger.

Ki looked around as the whistle sounded shrilly. He had heard the train before the whistle spoke, however. Or rather, he had felt it, felt its vibration underfoot, in the air. His senses were more finely tuned than those of most other men. His years of training had done that for him. *Te* had done it for him. All his life was structured around the martial arts, and the arts in turn had broadened his life, opening subtle windows in his mind. He heard and saw what others could

3

only guess at. He often *felt* movements and intentions. His body, Ki suspected, was closer to his spirit than were other men's.

The train chuffed its way into the Amarillo station, hissing and groaning, a porter standing ready with a cart, a man with a wooden step-down hanging on to the grab-rail of the Pullman.

Ki walked slowly along the platform. A few other people had come out of the depot to meet the arrivals: a tall man in range clothes, an older woman in balck, a drummer in a checked suit, looking anxiously up and down the platform, perhaps watching for the local law.

And the woman.

"Ki!" Jessica Starbuck called out, and Ki's heart warmed a little as he saw her. Her green eyes were wide with pleasure, and the sunlight glinted on her copper-blond hair, which just now was pinned up and pushed under a small green hat that matched the green traveling dress she wore.

He went to her and helped her down from the train. A tall man with reddish hair and a disappointed smile was behind Jessie, holding her luggage.

"Oh yes, thank you, Mr. Grant."

Ki took the luggage from the man, who had obviously hoped for a little more from his railroad romance.

"Perhaps if you're staying at the Texas House..." the young man began.

"I'm not sure where I'll be staying," Jessie said, "but thank you for the invitation." She smiled sweetly but definitely, and Mr. Grant, whatever his hopes had been, knew they had just been ended.

With Ki carrying the luggage, they walked quickly from the station. The sun beat down mercilessly. Amarillo was hot and dry, dust rising from the streets at each movement.

"Have you talked to them yet?" Jessie asked.

4

"The informer hasn't contacted Billings again. I've been looking around, but I haven't found anything. You would want to talk to Billings yourself."

"Yes," Jessie answered. She wanted very much to talk to Hank Billings.

After checking in at the State Hotel and taking the time to wash and change clothes, she did just that. Ki led her down the streets of Amarillo, toward the freight office where Hank Billings operated.

Heads turned to study Jessie Starbuck, whose light hair was now down, sunlit, shiny. Her figure was enough to attract men's eyes. She had on a white silk blouse that clung to her full, high breasts, and she wore a brown Stetson hat that dangled down her from its chin thong. She wore a green tweed skirt cinched with a wide belt.

Amarillo was growing wildly since the railroad had arrived. The smell of new green lumber was everywhere, the scent of sawdust, the sounds of hammering and sawing. The streets were filled with beer wagons and cowboys on the loose. To the south of town they were setting up tents for some sort of carnival, or perhaps it was a circus. Once, the strange, distant trumpeting of an elephant could be heard clearly above the general tumult.

"Here it is," Ki said.

Jessie looked up to see the freshly painted green and white sign: BILLINGS FREIGHT.

They pushed through the door into a crowded office, where a half-dozen perspiring men crowded around a desk behind which a harried little dispatcher worked.

"Is Mr. Billings in?" Jessie asked, and the chatter stopped as heads turned to find the source of the feminine voice.

"Is it Miss Starbuck?" the dispatcher asked.

"Yes."

"Mr. Billings is in. Go through the counter gate there

5

and through that door, please."

Jessie did, and just as Ki sometimes seemed to know things without seeing or hearing them, she knew that a half-dozen pairs of eyes were watching the switch of her nicely rounded bottom. Ki knew it as well, and he was surprised to discover that it irritated him. He had thought himself well past all that sort of useless emotion.

Hank Billings was a vast, redheaded, pink-cheeked man who smoked the foulest cigars Jessie had ever encountered.

He was affable and polite as well. "Miss Starbuck! I'll be! I can't believe it. I haven't seen you since you were a toddler, when old Alex was kind enough to have me down to his ranch... Well, those were better times. I was truly grieved when your father died."

"Thank you, Mr. Billings."

"Child, I'd be hurt if you didn't consent to call me Hank. Your... agent here, Mr. Ki, has already agreed to do that. We've become good friends in a short time, isn't that so, Mr. Ki?"

"Mr. Ki" nodded and stretched his mouth slightly in a mild smile of agreement. It satisfied "Hank," who was already talking about other things.

"The town is bustling, ain't it? I've got to admit that I'm doing all right... Sit down, please, Miss Starbuck. I've got to get off my feet and I can't rightly sag until you've sat down first. That's better, thank you. Yes." Billings went on, "I'm fine here. But it's not like the old days. Why, your father set me up, you know, like he set up a lot of folks. People remember him as a man who took things and kept them—and he did, too, railroads, mines, cattle ranches, shipping. Yes, he did that and he ran them fairly and turned a good profit, but there are a lot of us that just wasn't cut out to be another man's employee, and Alex Starbuck knew that, too. He got me started and then cut me loose on my

6

own. Finest man I ever knew," he said with a sad shake of his head.

"Ki tells me you have some important information for us," Jessie said, sitting back in the wooden chair.

"Yes. Did he fill you in much?"

"I'd like to hear it again. It's very important that we find these people."

"You're damned right it is—pardon me—but how is that gonna be done? The marshal doesn't care. Thinks I've popped my cork."

"The law can be very narrow," Ki put in.

"Don't I know it, Mr. Ki," Hank said with a sigh. "All right. I'll tell you what I know. You don't think these are the people that killed your father, do you?"

"I think there's a very strong chance," Jessie said.

"They'll be dangerous men, I'm thinking." Hank looked from Ki to Jessie and back again.

"If you'll just tell me what you know," Jessie said, and her smile lit up the room.

"Sure, sure," Hank Billings said. He had sagged into his chair and now he leaned back, steepling his fingers, his face half hidden behind the screen of tobacco smoke rising from the cigar poked into his mouth.

"It started when Jimbo Crest started yahooin' me one night—it's not important who he is, just a man who drinks too much and talks too much. He said he heard I'd missed the main chance, and when I asked him what he meant, he said, 'Why, that special trainload of goods that come in this afternoon, going west.'

"I didn't pay a lot of attention to Jimbo. Knowing him, there might not have been any special trainload of freight at all. Might've been needling me, you know. But I got to thinking about it. This is a competitive business, you know. There's half a dozen of us freighters in Amarillo now, and it might have been that someone was undercutting me. If they'd got a big job, I wanted to know, so I sent out a few feelers. Nothing," he said.

"What do you mean?" Jessie asked. She had taken off her hat and now she sat turning it on her lap, her green eyes studied Billings intently.

"Just nothing, Miss Starbuck. None of the competition would admit to any such shipment. A couple of them acted like I was loco. Any big shipment would have to be moved at night to avoid our greedy eyes." Hank laughed. "Yes sir, we keep an eye on each other," he told Ki, who nodded without expression.

"Didn't you ask at the railroad office?"

"Sure," Hank answered. "After a time, after it got to bothering me that someone in town had gotten a railroad car full of goods and moved them out under my nose without me even being aware of it."

"What did they tell you?" Jessie asked.

"They told me it wasn't my business!" He slapped his thigh in disbelief. "That's right. Not my business. Well, that damn well—pardon me—told me that there *had* been a shipment, all right. I thought, 'I'm losing business, but to who?' It wasn't normal for the competition not to gloat over a big deal they'd pulled off. Them boys like to rub your nose in it if they get the chance. Like I say, we're competitive, but real friendly in a way. Not that I'd back one of my crews off if they felt like cracking some Merriweather drivers' heads...Well, I guess you don't care about all of that in particular.

"Finally, just when I'd nearly gotten over it, a man shows up. At night. At my house."

"What did he look like?"

"Small man. Small shoulders. Big head. That's not much of a description, is it, but he kind of kept in the shadows,

8

you know. Standing on my porch, talking in a whispery voice."

"What did he say?"

"He says, 'I hear you're interested in a certain freight shipment and what became of it.'" Hank Billings stubbed out his cigar carefully. "I told him I was, maybe. I asked him what business was it of his. He said he was wise to the whole thing. Said he was a curious sort of fellow and had come across some interesting facts."

"Such as?" Jessie asked, leaning forward.

"Such as the shipment was firearms."

Ki and Jessie exchanged a glance. The shipment in question was an entire freightcar full of goods. That was a hell of a lot of weapons.

"What else did he say?"

"He said they were mostly new .44-40 Winchester repeating rifles. And then he hinted he would like to have a little money if he was to continue talking. I invited him in, but he was shy of the light, it seems. I went into the house and got him some cash. Twenty dollars, it seems to me. I was interested, yes. There's been a lot of Comanche trouble over west, and I thought, 'Well, if someone I'm in competition with is selling those rifles to the Comanches, I'd better damn well find out."

"But it wasn't the Comanches."

"The little man said not, but then his story was so incredible that I stuck to my own idea for a long while. I figured either the little man was lying to me or someone had been joshing him."

"What was his story?" Jessie asked.

"It went like this," Hank Billings said, leaning forward intently, hands clasped. "There's a man over the line in New Mexico Territory, by name Ray Cheney. Cheney is a man with big ideas, it seems. His idea at the present time

9

is to take a good-sized chunk of the territory and make it his own. Make his own empire on American soil, get me?"

"I do," Jessie said.

"Crazy, I say," Billings threw in.

"Not necessarily," Ki said. "New Mexico Territory is a long way from Washington, just as Texas was once a long way from Mexico City. Nations are formed through force of arms and legitimized through them."

"Yeah." Billings nodded his dubious agreement. "Maybe, but it would take a hell of a lot of force of arms to take a whole territory away from the United States."

"Yes," Ki answered quietly.

"If I were going to try it, I know how I'd go about it," Jessie told them. "First secede, then attach myself temporarily to a foreign power—Spain, Mexico, or France would do. Later I could worry about cutting those tethers. Meanwhile, I'd have a sponsor."

"That's Alex Starbuck's daughter," Billings laughed. "She knows how to build an empire."

"They still need many guns and men," Ki said. "We assume they now have the guns."

"The guns haven't left Amarillo yet," Billings answered. "Not according to the little man. They're leaving on the fourteenth. Day after tomorrow."

"But we don't know who's handling the shipment or where it's bound."

"No."

"Or who's behind it," Ki said cautiously, glancing again at Jessie, whose mouth had tightened a little.

"*Do* we know?" Jessie asked.

"I don't know a thing, just what the little man said," Billings said, and went on, "He told me this much: for soldiers, Cheney has gotten in touch with Chato Cruz—heard of him, have you? Butcher, he is, wanted both sides

10

of the border, and rightly. He kills anything he doesn't like. Age and sex make no difference to him. He's plenty mean, without scruples or loyalties."

"The perfect revolutionary," Jessie put in. She brushed back a long, loose strand of blond hair.

"Jessie needs to hear the rest of it," Ki said. "It is at that point that our interests begin to have something in common."

"Yeah, right," Billings sighed. "Well, according to my informant, there's a foreign power behind this—not too much removed from your speculation, Miss Starbuck—not a nation, however; 'a group of businessmen' was how it was put to me. People with big money and big power, people who don't mind killing for what they want."

Jessie just sat looking at Billings, at the wall behind him. She knew who it was. It felt right. There was no one else with the power, money, or guts to try something like this.

The cartel had moved in again—a hungry, grasping octopus that was everywhere, seeking more power, more wealth to feed on. It was intent on destroying America's economy in order to annex it, intent on bleeding the country dry. It did not balk even at murder, as Jessie knew only too well.

Her father had begun in the import-export business. In the Orient and in San Francisco he had collided with the cartel. During a series of bloody trade wars, Jessie's mother had died at the cartel's hands. Later they had finished the job by assassinating her father, leaving the empire, the grief, and the job of retribution to Jessie.

"What else did your informant say?"

"That was it. How much of it can we believe?" Billings asked. He was trying to smile, but it didn't work out.

"Too much, I'm afraid."

"Yes," Billings said, shrugging as if there were a great weight resting on his shoulders. "Say, there was one other

11

thing. This man mentioned an imported killer. A gunfighter or what, I don't know. But he was being sent from Europe to take charge of things here."

"Yes?" Ki was interested. A frown cut two deep, parallel lines between his dark eyebrows.

"Yeah, his name was the Angel, something like that. The Death Angel, yeah, that was it!"

The Death Angel. Ki looked at Jessie, but she had not heard the name before. Ki had. Not much was known physically of the Death Angel. Ki had heard he was European, but whether fair or dark, tall or short, he did not know. But he was good, he was very good. Like Ki, the Death Angel had studied in the Orient; he too had been nurtured by the masters of the martial arts. He worked for the cartel now, did he?

"So," Billings said, rising, "that's it, I'm afraid. Miss Starbuck. The little man is supposed to come back tonight. He's supposed to tell me how the arms are traveling, what their destination is, and how to recognize this Death Angel gent. But you know how these people are, these hangers-on, these people who try to play both sides. He got his twenty dollars from me. I doubt he'll be back."

"Where were you supposed to meet him?"

"Near the railroad water tank. A quarter-mile outside the east end of town, on the tracks."

"At what time?"

"Midnight. Say, Miss Starbuck, you think I ought to show up?"

"No," Jessie said, shaking her head vigorously so that her reddish gold hair swirled and floated around her face. *"I'm* going to do that, Mr. Billings. I want to thank you for what you've done."

"It was nothing, really." He showed them out of his

12

office. "But it might be a little dangerous to go out and meet that little man tonight."

"It might be," Jessie agreed. And Billings looked into her green eyes and Ki's black ones, and just nodded. If these two couldn't handle it, then he couldn't either.

There was nothing left to say but "Good luck," and Billings did that, watching as the pretty blonde and the tall man walked out of his office and into trouble.

Chapter 2

Ki had driven the wagon to Amarillo. High, enclosed, equipped with a variety of essential materiel, from Ki's spare clothes to his deadly assortment of weapons, such as his *sai*, his *jo*, his *surushin*—a sort of primitive *bolas*, a rope with weights on either end, which Ki sometimes wore disguised as a belt and which was deadly and silent as were most of his weapons, excluding the *nage teppò* grenades that rested in a small drawer, and the very modern, very noisy crate of dynamite.

Ki's life's work was combat. He was as well trained and well equipped for it as any man can be. Now the half-Japanese man stood in the wagon, watching Jessie, who had seated herself in a wooden chair bolted to the floor of the wagon.

"It is them," she said aloud.

"Yes. Of course."

"Then we've got to stop it. We've got to stop the arms shipment if possible. That won't be enough, though, will it, Ki?" Jessie looked up at her companion, adviser, and protector.

"No."

"It won't stop them. They'll just get more arms somewhere else."

"Did the government not understand the real threat here?" Ki wondered. "This country is very young, not yet stabilized. Its borders change each decade. Do they not understand that the borders can retract as well as expand?"

"I don't think they understand that, no. We *are* a young country," Jessie said, "and like a young person, we only see growth and achievement ahead, not failure or decay."

"Someone must be informed, someone who will listen."

"I agree." Both were thinking of Marshal Custis Long. He would listen, he would believe. But who knew where he was now? "We'll try to get some government help, but meanwhile we haven't much time. The arms are supposed to leave the day after tomorrow. Have you had time to check the other carriers?"

"No. From what Billings told us, it seems a waste of time."

"It probably is, but we'd better do it anyway. I'd like to talk to the local marshal, too. Have you seen him?"

"His name is Caffiter. He doesn't seem interested in much but alcohol."

"I want to see him anyway. See if you can find out anything from the other freight outfits. Also, check the stables and see if anyone has rented a large number of wagons. They may have hired one here, another there." She shrugged.

"And then tonight you wish me to meet the informant at the water tower."

"Tonight we go together," Jessie said positively. She rose and put on her hat. "Supper at the hotel?"

"Yes," Ki said without enthusiasm. He never found much of interest on hotel menus.

Jessie went out then into the bright yellow glare of the

15

day. She started uptown, through the dust and confusion, toward the marshal's office, which was a low adobe building on the main street. The man behind the desk wore a tarnished brass star on his red shirt. He looked at Jessie and started to rise, then apparently decided it was too much trouble, for he sagged back to rake Jessie with his pouched brown eyes, a whisper of a smile on his whiskered face.

"Yes'm?"

"Are you the marshal?"

The man was amused by the question. "No'm. Marshal Caffiter, he would be at the Savage Trails."

"A saloon?"

"A tea garden, ma'am," the deputy said sardonically.

"Where," Jessie asked, holding back her temper, "is the Savage Trails, exactly?"

"It's the red building around the corner, ma'am. Where all the hooting will be going on."

"And what does Marshal Caffiter look like?"

"Ma'am, he'll be the one doing the hooting."

The deputy snickered, and Jessie gave it up. She went on out into the sunlight, feeling hot, sticky, and weary although it was relatively early. The train ride hadn't been exactly refreshing. There had been a fire in the freight car behind Jessie's Pullman, when sparks from the stack had touched tinder-dry wood and paint. They had stopped to put the fire out, and the entire train had been wreathed in acrid smoke.

The Savage Trails was a barn-shaped, barn-colored building. It was indeed filled with hooting drunks. Jessie pushed on through the batwing doors.

Everything inside the Savage Trails was in motion. Hip-swinging saloon girls moved across the floor with trays of drinks, the roulette wheel spun on the table to Jessie's left, cards fluttered from the hands of the dealer to the cowboys and townsmen gathered around the green felt tables. Behind the bar, the bartender poured and scooped up change. The piano player banged at an instrument with two keys missing, the rest in shocking disharmony.

Everything didn't stop as Jessie entered, but for a moment it seemed as though things did. The bartender stopped pouring. Heads at the bar turned toward her. The cardplayers muttered. The saloon girls hissed to each other. The piano player missed a beat. The roulette wheel kept on spinning, but Jocko Brown, who had been playing red for ten turns without winning, finally won and he didn't even notice it.

"Look at that! Damn me, *that* is a woman!" he shouted.

"No ladies in here," the bartender said.

"You got women in here," Jessie shot back, inclining her head toward the saloon girls, who wore bright, low-cut dresses.

"Them ain't *ladies*," the bartender replied.

Jessie ignored the man. She looked around, spotted the man with the silver star on his faded blue shirt, and started that way while the motion in the saloon gradually picked up again. Heads followed her silently as she crossed the room, and once or twice she heard a low whistle of approval.

"Marshal Caffiter?"

She stood over him, and slowly a massive head with gray sidewhiskers, a veined nose, and jowled cheeks lifted to her.

"He ain't here."

"Marshal Caffiter, my name is Jessie Starbuck."

"Starbuck?" the marshal shook his head as if confused. "Heard that name before somewhere."

"Do you mind if I sit down?" Jessie asked. She pulled out a chair opposite the marshal. His booted feet dropped from it and thumped against the floor. Caffiter poured another drink, sipped at it, and sat rubbing his raw-meat-colored face. There was some sort of minor commotion behind Jessie, but she didn't bother to glance back. There was always some sort of minor commotion in a place like this.

"Still here?" Caffiter asked sleepily. When Jessie answered, it was with a touch of annoyance.

"What do the people of this town pay you for, anyway? Yes, I'm still here. I have a problem and I need some help." Caffiter didn't reply. "There's a large shipment of illegal arms headed for New Mexico Territory out of Amarillo. A man named Chato Cruz is going to end up with those guns. I know you've heard of him."

"If he ain't in Amarillo, I don't care what he does," Caffiter said.

Jessie was beginning to wonder whose relative Caffiter was. He couldn't have been elected on his ability; as far as she could see, he had none. He was able to pour a drink, however, and he did that again as Jessie watched.

Behind her the commotion had built to a scraping and cussing. She glanced across her shoulder to see a tall man with a stringy mustache and a cruel little expression shove. What he had shoved was a redheaded saloon girl. She spun away, crashing into the table. She shrieked and then slid to the floor, toppling the table, and with it cards and poker chips, glasses and bottles.

"You lousy bitch," the man with the mustache said. The woman just sat on the floor in a puddle of beer, crying.

Jessie looked to the marshal, expecting him to rise and do something. Even him.

But he didn't. He sat there drinking, and the tall man with the mustache swung a chair out of his way and stepped toward the girl on the floor. No one paid any attention to the marshal's presence. No one seemed to care, and apparently that was the way Caffiter wanted it.

18

"You'd cross me, would you, you little slut!" the tall man said, and Jessie got to her feet, filling her hand with the little derringer from behind her belt.

"Leave her alone," she said, and for the second time that afternoon she halted the processes of the saloon in their tracks, brought the mustached man to a dead stop, and quieted the raucous hooting. This time the piano player even stopped.

"What did you say?" the man with the mustache asked, his eyes scanning Jessie up and down, halting at waist level, where the twin over-and-under muzzles of the little derringer watched him back.

"Leave her alone," Jessie said. She wasn't afraid, but she was uneasy. The man was mad drunk, drunk enough to not give a damn whether he was shot or not. "Just back off, mister, and get back to your whiskey. Leave the woman alone."

The girl on the floor was looking up at Jessie with dark, frightened eyes. Her makeup was smeared and streaked with tears. She was quivering with fear.

The big man just laughed. "Why don't you just shoot and we'll see what happens!" His words were slurred, but his intent was clear. He took a step forward and Jessie drew back the hammer of her pistol.

It was then that the other man acted. Just what he did, Jessie wasn't sure afterward. She saw a blond man with broad shoulders, wearing a pale blue shirt, move in. She saw his knee lift, his hand shoot out, and then the drunk was down on the floor beside the woman he had put there. He was facedown in the pool of beer, his eyes rolled back, his limbs twitching slightly. He was out cold, and he was going to be for a long while.

"Sorry for butting in," the blond man said to Jessie. "But it seemed preferable to having you shoot him."

19

"It was that," Jessie said. "But..." But what had he done to him? The man's movements had been quick, difficult to define. His hands had made tiny butterfly motions around the drunk's head and he had fallen. Just fallen.

"I'm Quayle, John Quayle," the blond man said. "Are you ready to leave?"

"Yes." Jessie looked around. The marshal was still at his whiskey. "I guess so." She smiled and John Quayle returned it. His smile was confident, appealing even. He gave Jessie his arm and they walked out into the heated day.

"Where are you staying?" Quayle asked.

"Why?"

"I thought you'd want to go there. I was going to escort you, that's all."

"I don't need an escort," Jessie said. But if she did, this wouldn't be a bad one for the job. His face was tanned and handsome, his eyes very blue. Holding his arm as they left the saloon, she had felt the knotted muscle there, the taut sinews.

"I guess you don't." Quayle smiled again. "I just hate to say goodbye so soon."

"We'll have to for now, I'm afraid."

"But you didn't tell me where you were staying."

"No. I didn't."

Quayle was able to take a hint. He bade Jessie good day and walked away up the boardwalk. And she stood a moment studying his rolling gait, his slim hips and broad shoulders, feeling just a little bit like a fool for running him off.

But there was something strange about the man—nothing she could name or even guess at. There was something that did not *feel* right with John Quayle. But then maybe she had been on the road too long, enmeshed in too many conspiracies and intrigues. Maybe she had gotten to where she did not trust people, and if that was so, it was a shame. Her father, she recalled, had once told her that to feel that way was was deadly.

"I have been burned, Jessie," Alex Starbuck had said. He had been sitting at the massive desk in the study on the ranch. Jessie had been a small girl, and angry at someone— she couldn't recall now what had precipitated the conversation. She remembered her father strongly, however, the room with its fine leather furniture, the gleaming glass-windowed cabinets filled with firearms, the scent of his cherry pipe tobacco. "I've been burned many times, girl. Sometimes when I knew going in that I was liable to get burned. But you can't mistrust everyone. We only have people to believe in, and if they are all nothing, well, it makes us just that much less ourselves. Sometimes you have to trust, even if it hurts."

She walked slowly back toward the hotel, knowing now that she wasn't going to get any help from the local law. Not that Caffiter would have been able to do that much, but it was his area, and he at least knew the people.

Ki was not in the wagon. He was still out checking the stables and freighters, apparently. Jessie went on into the hotel and up to her room, relishing the opportunity to lie down on a real bed. She lay on the bed and indulged in real sleep.

Ki was wide awake and annoyed. He was annoyed because the two men had been following him most of the afternoon, and they still were. He was annoyed because it was going to lead to trouble, and there was no point in trouble just now. But they weren't going to leave him any choice.

"Hey, China boy!" the darker one shouted again, as Ki turned off the main street and walked back along an alley toward the grove of cottonwood trees beyond. Ki's mouth tightened a little; he should have been above it, but he was piqued at being called Chinese.

"Wait for us, China boy!"

Ki couldn't decide whether he had some of the usual town trash in his wake, or whether these were men with an actual mission.

The former seemed more likely, although Ki had spent the day looking for the freight handler who had transported the weapons, and if someone in that line was connected with the cartel, he would have had time to hire local talent and put them on Ki's trail.

"Wait up, boy!" the redheaded one called as Ki reached the trees. With a sigh, Ki turned and watched the approach of the two swaggering bullies. He glanced around and saw that they were alone in the trees, that they could not be observed from any side. It seemed to suit the thugs as well as it did Ki. They came on, jostling each other, snickering.

"Did you want to speak to me?" Ki asked with just a little weariness. Why was the world so glutted with men like this?

"Don't he talk nice for a China boy?" the dark one said. "Hell, yes, we want to talk to you. Tall China boy, ain't he, Red?"

"He's tall. Gives him a long way to fall," Red answered. He had his thumbs hooked in his belt, a stub of cigarette dangling from his lips. It was, Ki thought, a horribly inept way to make ready for battle—and that was what they were doing. Now Ki could read it in their eyes—in the dull, watery eyes of the dark one, which wriggled a little, as if there were snakes coiling and uncoiling in their depths. And in the faded blue eyes of the redhead. Yes, they had come to hurt. They were half drunk and they liked pushing. Ki nearly felt bad about this. He tried to talk them out of it.

"People get hurt when they fight. Getting hurt is unpleasant."

22

"See, didn't I tell you he talked pretty?" the dark one said, and he lifted a hand to shove at Ki's shoulder. A sudden, stabbing pain knifed through his arm. The "China-man" had taken his hand and was squeezing it, folding it back against its wrist, his fingers digging into nerves. The thug yelled and stepped back.

"Please," Ki said, but they had been paid, and they were going to take it seriously.

The redheaded man jumped at him, a knife flashing in his hand. Ki stepped to meet him and blocked the clumsy attempt easily with a *gedenpbarai,* or downward block. The redhead blinked and then choked as Ki's forked fingers stabbed at his throat, flanking the Adam's apple. He could just as easily have crushed the larynx with that blow. The redheaded man fell back, strangling. The other one hadn't learned his lesson yet. He had his pistol out, and he thrust it toward Ki's belly. Ki slapped the pistol to one side with his left hand, and quicker than the eye could follow he executed a *yonhon-nukite-uchi,* a spear-hand thrust to the bully's abdomen. Stiffened fingers stabbed into the dark-eyed man's belly, just above his gleaming belt buckle. The blow was a good one. Nerves were paralyzed, wind forced violently from the man's body. The thug folded up and sagged to his knees, his pistol falling free. The redhead was still gaping at Ki, who turned again to face him, his legs slightly bent, his hands rising in front of his eyes like writh-ing cobras. The redhead took off at a dead run. The dark one lay on the ground, vomiting. Now he got up shakily, still holding his belly. He looked at Ki as if for permission, then rose and staggered away, leaving his gun behind.

Ki didn't smile. There was nothing amusing about men trying to kill you. Either of those plug-uglies could have done the job, as clumsy as they were. They too could have died if Ki had intended to kill them.

Ki let them go, but a minute later he regretted not having

23

asked who had sent them. It didn't matter, he supposed. If they had come on their own, they would not be back. If they had been sent, then someone else would come. Maybe someone very good. Maybe the best. Maybe the Death Angel.

Chapter 3

In the hour before midnight, Amarillo was running wild, like a cheap clock with its mainspring overwound. There was shouting and fighting, a woman's scream, the sound of glass breaking, and once a shot, distant, muffled, followed by a moment's deep silence.

"It is an odd way to choose to live," Ki said reflectively. He stood at the window of Jessie's hotel room, watching the dark streets below.

"It was meant to be an easier way." Jessie finished brushing her hair and stood. She was wearing her more businesslike gun on this night—a peachwood-handled double-action .38 Colt, mounted on a .44 frame. She wore denim jeans and a matching jacket.

Even with Ki along, it seemed like a good idea to carry the Colt to a midnight meeting with an informant. Ki was still following his thought about towns.

"They gather together for safety, and yet here there is much less safety than on the open plains. They live close together, but instead of treating each other with an additional courtesy that crowding demands, they become rude and aggressive."

"It's not like that in Japan, is it?"

"No. It's an older and wiser culture, Jessie."

"I can't figure out what all those people are doing in the middle of the night." Jessie came up beside Ki, and he could smell the soap cleanness of her. He glanced at her and then looked deliberately away.

"They drink. They throw away their money."

"What's that, south of town?" Jessie asked, indicating a glow of light above the buildings.

"The circus. I wonder that a traveling circus can do well in this part of the country, where towns are so far apart."

"We haven't much time. Do you want to get started?"

"Yes. I think so." Ki was frowning now, and Jessie, who had half turned away, looked back.

"What is it?"

"I don't know. For a moment I thought I saw someone down there in the shadows."

"Where?"

"He's gone now."

"One of those men you were telling me about?" she asked.

"I don't think so. This one has quiet feet. He moves easily. Those two were clumsy."

"Ki, this...this Death Angel. Is he good?"

Ki gazed out the window a moment before answering. "Very good. Also cold and without mercy."

"I haven't heard of him before. I know I never saw his name—at least not *that* name—in Alex's book."

The book to which she referred was a leatherbound ledger in a secret compartment in her father's desk back at the Circle Star Ranch. It was a list of cartel operatives and their connections, which Alex Starbuck had begun compiling many years before, and which Jessie had continued to correct and update after her father's death. There was another copy, a smaller, condensed version, which Jessie carried with her when she traveled. This one was kept in a private code that only Jessie could read.

"I don't believe he would be in Alex's book," Ki replied. "But sometimes one...hears things. The Death Angel is said to be a man with almost supernatural talent, one who has absorbed all the skills of *jujutsu, atemi, kenjutsu*—but he uses them only to kill, disdaining their use as a means of understanding oneself. They say he even killed his own teacher, the Chinese master Lo Fan."

"Isn't it odd that he should be connected with this business? What could the cartel have in mind, to send him here?"

Ki turned slowly and looked at Jessie. "The cartel knows we are here, and it knows why. The Death Angel has been sent to kill me."

Jessie was silent for a moment, then she nodded and said, "Please be careful, Ki."

"Come on," he said. "It's time we were going."

Jessie turned down the lamp and they opened the hall door. The tall man with the blond hair stood there, his face shadowed by his hatbrim.

"Hello, Miss Starbuck," John Quayle said.

"God! You startled me. What are you doing here?"

"I thought maybe you'd like to go down to the dining room for a cup of coffee." Quayle's placid, pale eyes flowed over Jessie's body and she found herself liking their caress. Quayle glanced at Ki and nodded curtly. Jessie introduced the two men. Neither offered to shake hands.

"It's too late for anything like that," Jessie said, aware of the incongruity, since she was just going out.

"We haven't much time," Ki put in.

"Am I keeping you?" Quayle asked.

"What made you think of coming up at this time of night?" Jessie asked.

Quayle smiled distantly. "I knew you were up. I saw your light. I was watching your window from across the street," he said unashamedly.

Ki was studying the man, liking and yet distrusting the calm sureness in his blue eyes. Was it this one who had been watching from across the street? This one who moved like a cat?

"We really do have to be going," Jessie said. "We have a late business meeting."

"All right." Quayle smiled and stepped aside. "I'm sorry. I was hoping we could spend some time together."

"Another time, maybe," Jessie answered, and there was just a hint of interest in her voice. Ki nodded again, and they walked past John Quayle and down the corridor. When they reached the stairs, Ki glanced back. Quayle still stood there, watching after them.

"Who is that?" he asked on the way down the darkened stairs.

Jessie told him about the saloon brawl. "That's all I know of him. Why?"

"I don't know why. There is something about him . . . He is a trained athlete, a man who uses his body knowingly." And what did that mean? Nothing. Ki shrugged off the concerns that nagged at him. Such worries were for old women. Perhaps after they had a chance to talk to the informant, they would know more about Mr. John Quayle.

They had decided to walk to the water tower east of town, and they did that, following the twin steel rails that gleamed blue and silver in the starlight. An owl followed them for a way, diving once, clicking sounds issuing from its throat. The city sounds faded, and the night silence descended like a shroud.

They could see the water tank silhouetted against the starry sky now, and they veered away from the railroad tracks, moving through the willow brush that thrived around the tower, watered by the spills and leakage.

There wasn't more than a quarter of an hour until midnight, but there was no sign of anyone, no out-of-place sound. They positioned themselves near the water tower, in the brush. The shadow cast by the tank lay over them. Ki stilled his breath and listened.

He could detect nothing, nothing at all. He had been watching behind them as they walked to the tower, trusting nothing, no one. The blond man was still on his mind, as well. He may have been an ardent admirer of Jessie's, nothing more. But to stand and watch a window at that time of night was not usual.

Jessie was thinking about the tall man as well, but her thoughts were a little warmer than Ki's. She liked him, liked his pale eyes, broad smile, square shoulders, and long legs. She wasn't foolish enough to overlook his odd behavior, and although John Quayle's explanation was flattering enough, it seemed inadequate.

She returned her attention to the night surrounding them, to the shadows cast by the willows, to the cleared area around the railroad water tank, to the tank itself, tall, massive, smelling of water and creosote.

It was Jessie who spoke:

"He won't be telling us anything."

"He may yet come," Ki whispered.

"He's here, but he won't be telling us anything. Look." She pointed, and then Ki too saw the dark, inert form slumped at the base of one of the water tank's supporting uprights.

They started forward together. Jessie had her Colt in her hand. Ki's eyes searched the shadows, finding nothing. The little man lay still and dead in the night.

They rolled him over, seeing nothing but a small, blank-

29

looking face, the eyes wide to the night sky, the lips parted. There was no visible wound.

"Is this him?"

"It must be. The description matches. Who else would be out here?"

"Has he anything to tell us?" Ki asked. "The dead speak sometimes."

"I don't think this one has much to say."

Ki was going through the man's pockets. As he moved him, he noticed the lack of rigidity. The man hadn't been dead long, not long at all. With practiced hands he ran over the body, examining bones and cartilage. He couldn't find the cause of death, and it worried him.

"Maybe it was an accident. His heart?" Jessie suggested.

"A strange coincidence, if so," Ki said. He shook his head. "No, I can't accept that."

Neither could Jessie, really. She watched Ki examine the body, feeling let down and empty. This one knew something. He could have opened doors to them.

The pale moon was rising now, its faint sheen glossing the plains. By that light Jessie did a little investigating of her own.

"Ah. Very skilled," Ki said. He lit a match and looked more closely at the small spot of blood on the eyeball of the dead man.

"Did you find it?"

"A wire through the eye socket," Ki told her. "Very nearly undetectable. Very sure."

"Do you have another match?"

Ki found one in his vest and struck it with his thumbnail. It flared up brightly, orange and blue woven together momentarily until it paled to a dull yellow.

"What is it?"

"There's something on his neck. Here, and here," Jessie indicated. "Do you see."

Ki nodded and touched the white smears. "What is it?"

"Greasepaint."

"Are you sure?" The match flickered out.

"Oh yes," Jessie answered. "It's—" Her head came up and she half turned, looking into the darkness. Ki was crouched and alert. He had heard it too. There was someone out there.

"Let's go," Ki said. "There's nothing more to be learned here."

It seemed judicious. They started back toward Amarillo, seeing the pale glow of its few late-burning lights against the sky. There was no one following them, but each of them carried an inexplicable uneasy feeling.

"The way he was killed," Jessie said, when they were well away from the tower. "It was someone with special skills who did the job."

"Yes. Special skills or a rich imagination. I've heard of a Chinese sect that disposes of its enemies in a similar way, but I've never seen murder done by that means."

"Our informant was an actor," Jessie said. "How would an actor come to know about the arms shipment and the land-grab scheme?"

"I don't know, but he was not as clever as he thought, unfortunately for him."

"An actor." The thought bothered Jessie. She had taken three more steps before she halted abruptly and looked at Ki, who had been struck by the same idea at the same time.

"Yes. The circus."

"It would have many wagons with it," Jessie commented. "Enough to carry any amount of contraband, perhaps." If the marshal could be persuaded to search the circus grounds ... but that was very unlikely, knowing Caffiter.

"It won't do us any good to go there tonight, and it could be exceptionally dangerous."

"But in the morning..."

31

"In the morning," Ki agreed.

It had to be the circus, Jessie thought. She had wondered how that outfit meant to make money this far west, where days of uncertain travel separated towns, where they were liable to suffer Indian attacks, drought, breakdowns. Maybe they had found a way to make it profitable. And if it involved murder—well, nothing came cheap.

They separated at the hotel. Jessie still wanted that bed while she could use it. Ki preferred to be in the wagon anyway. Jessie went on up the silent stairway to the second floor and her room.

There was someone in there.

She knew it as soon as she opened the door. Whether it was scent or sound, or some other, more subtle sense that informed her mind of another presence, the warning came none too soon.

Jessie threw herself to one side as the tall figure appeared, outlined starkly against the window behind him. He reached for Jessie, and her Colt exploded flame. The intruder screamed with pain as the bullet from Jessie's pistol struck him high on the shoulder and half turned him around.

The man leaped for the door and was through it before Jessie could fire again. She went out into the corridor after him, but she saw only a dark figure rounding the corner of the corridor.

"What was that?" demanded a man who stuck his head out the door of the next room. "Someone get shot, lady?"

"I don't know. It must have been on the other side."

Jessie went back in her room. There was no point in waiting to talk to the marshal—if he ever came—or in standing around discussing the incident with a bunch of strangers. She walked to the window, saw Ki looking up, and made a sign that everything was all right. Then she kicked off her boots and stripped down, climbing naked

32

between the sheets to lie awake thinking about a dead man, a midnight intruder—and a tall blond man with broad shoulders and a pleasant smile, with strong hands, a deep chest, and bright blue eyes...

After an early breakfast, Ki and Jessie headed for the big tents pitched on the south side of town. They could hear a variety of morning sounds—big cats growling, elephants trumpeting, monkeys chattering, all expecting and demanding food.

They passed a very pretty Indian girl leading three matched white horses to water. Farther on, a family of midgets was having coffee around a fire built in a tin stove.

"What is it you hope to find?" Ki asked. "The weapons, if there are any, are well concealed. We can't tear the circus apart."

"No. But keep your eyes open for a man with a bullet hole in his shoulder."

"You think your burglar works here?"

"The dead man did."

They wandered through the circus, which was larger than either of them expected, strolling past game booths, animal cages, acrobats in bright clothing.

"Many people. Many hiding places," Ki observed.

"This has to be it." She was still not positive. She was trying to convince herself, but it didn't take a lot to do that. A skinny man with a leather cap was leading an elephant past, holding it by the ear.

"Excuse me," Jessie said. "How many shows today?"

"Three," the skinny man said with some surprise. He blinked in the bright sun, and the elephant's trunk curled around him like a great gray snake in an affectionate gesture.

"And tomorrow?"

"Why, tomorrow we pull out," the elephant handler said.

33

"So soon?"

"Lady, it's been a week. Tomorrow's the fourteenth already. It's all writ on them posters that are plastered all over town."

With that the man went on, the elephant shuffling behind him, lifting a wake of dry dust.

"What was that?" Ki wanted to know.

"The fourteenth. That's when the informant said the arms were leaving."

"So it is." Ki nodded thoughtfully. "And what do we do now?"

"Now?" Jessie smiled brightly. "Did you ever want to be in the circus, Ki?"

"Jessie..." Ki began.

"Why not? It's the only way we're going to learn anything."

"I dislike making a spectacle of myself," Ki said, but already he knew they were going. It was the logical step. Logical, if highly dangerous. There was someone with the circus who liked to kill and did it skillfully. They passed hundreds of people, any one of whom could be the killer. Or the Death Angel. Would he be here as well? Of course. He would be watching over the shipment. It was logical, in fact, to assume that it was the Death Angel who had killed the informer.

"Miss Starbuck!"

Jessie's head came around and her smile deepened. It was John Quayle, but not the same man she had met in town. This one wore gold-colored tights that fit his muscular body tightly. He strode toward them, his smile deeply pleased. Jessie noticed with relief that Quayle certainly didn't have an injured shoulder.

"What are you doing here?" Quayle asked. He took both of Jessie's hands and she let him.

"Looking around, the same as everyone else."

"It's hours until anything is open."

"But you," she said, stepping back to look him over. "What are you doing here?"

"I live here."

"And work here?"

"Yes. I'm a trapeze man. High wire as well. My sister and I have been doing it since we were five and six years old." He shrugged, as if it weren't an interesting story, and looked into Jessie's eyes. "You'll be at the first performance today?"

"Yes. Yes," she said, "I'll be here."

"Look for me, then." A hand swept down his costumed body. "I'll be wearing this." Quayle nodded to Ki. "Nice to see you again, too."

Ki grunted something in response, and stood, arms folded, looking around as Jessie and the acrobat said goodbye. He had still carried some hope that they could continue their investigation without joining the circus themselves. Now Ki looked at Jessie, at the glow on her cheeks as she watched the tall blond man walk away. They were, Ki knew, going to become a part of the big show. He was not pleased.

Chapter 4

They wandered the grounds as the day warmed and the people from Amarillo began to saunter down, as the booths and games began to open for business, as the steam organ down near the big tent began to toot, and the clowns, with their makeup on, strolled and gamboled and tumbled through the crowd.

"It's impossible to find a wounded man among them," Ki said. "And if the wound was very serious, he'll be somewhere else, in a wagon perhaps. There is a row of wagons near the trees that are obviously living quarters. Perhaps if I went down that way I could discover something."

"If you want to. I'm going to try to find the manager's wagon, or whatever he uses for an office."

"Jessie," Ki said, and there was some sternness in his tone, "I will not put on a red nose and dance around."

She laughed and placed a hand on his arm. "Don't worry, there'll be something else for you to do."

"Where shall I meet you?"

"There." She nodded toward a red and gilt wagon, where

36

a man sold tickets for the main show. "I'll get two tickets and meet you there at one o'clock."

Ki nodded and went off through the throng. He was comfortable there, in an odd sort of way. He didn't stand out so obviously among the circus people. He saw immensely fat people, and a man well over seven feet tall and thin as a wheat stalk; another walked by on stilts, towering over Ki. Along the midway he saw women in spangles and veils, dancing, their bellies undulating, bells on their fingers tinkling. His eyes combed the crowd, the attractions, searching for an injured man, searching for one who might be the Death Angel, finding nothing suspicious.

The wheezing of the steam organ died away as he walked toward the circle of wagons beneath the trees. It was much like a gypsy encampment, Ki thought. Many of the men and women he passed were southern Europeans or Asians. Turkish eyes followed him without interest as he walked through the trees, hearing the dogs barking, seeing the young children at play.

Ki walked through the wagon circle now, and his eyes were alert. The midnight burglar had taken a bullet from Jessie's gun, there was no doubt about that. The hotel room was spattered with blood. If the guns were with the circus, as they believed, the attacker was also here. Ki meant to find him.

He halted, stepped quickly behind the mottled trunk of a huge sycamore tree, and stood watching, a frown drawing his eyebrows together.

A woman was standing at a boiling pot of water, rinsing white cloth in it. There were stains on the cloth, which appeared dark maroon from where Ki stood in the shadows of the trees. He couldn't see the woman's face, but he could see by her quick, nervous movements that she was agitated.

She turned toward the green wagon behind her and walked

37

that way, carrying clean clothes. Ki slipped through the shadows, following. He could hear nothing from inside the wagon. He approached cautiously, moving toward the front of the wagon, where there was a small window. Stepping onto the ledge beneath the window, he chinned himself and peered in.

The woman must have felt the wagon move, and she intuitively looked to the window. Her dark, almond-shaped eyes met Ki's as he peered into the dark interior, and she screamed, "What do you want! Get out of there, you dirty man! Filthy thing!"

Ki, who had had his brief look inside, enough to reveal that the woman was alone in there, dropped to the ground. She was already out the door, down the steps, charging at him with a broomstick.

She was Chinese, Ki saw. She was also enraged, offended, and very pretty. Diminutive and nicely molded, with pert, uptilted breasts outlined clearly beneath her white shirt.

Ki had a split second to notice that before she began flailing at him with the broom handle. He ducked to the left, stepped to the right, shifted his body to one side and then to the other, and the Chinese woman, panting angrily, missed him four times, yelling in Cantonese all the while.

"Stand still, white demon, so that I may strike you. Aya!" she pointed an accusing finger. "Not only white, Japanese! I know it. Japanese!" She made a very loud, very disgusted noise and tried again to hit Ki. She tried, but she was tiring and she contented herself with grumbling and chattering in Chinese after three more attempts.

"I am very sorry," Ki said in her language. it didn't seem prudent to explain why he had to peek in her window, even if she gave him the chance. But she didn't.

"Japanese devil!" she shrieked again. Her long, silky black hair flew around her face like a dark mist as she gave

38

it one last try, lifting the broom handle with two hands, hacking down at Ki as if she were chopping firewood. Ki easily stepped aside, and with a short bow of apology he turned and walked away, her screamed insults following him.

Once he stopped and looked back and thought that he had never been hated by anyone he found quite so attractive.

Jessie wandered through the circus grounds, working her way toward the north end of the midway, where the manager's office was housed in a small, undistinguished wagon. It was the last day for the circus in Amarillo, but many of the people must have come back for a second or even a third visit, for the grounds were crowded with men, women, and children.

There were lines in front of the fortune-teller's tent, and lines at the sideshows, where a barker shouted out the attractions to be found inside, such as Lulu, the Fattest Woman in the World, and Jojo, the Dogfaced Boy.

The manager's wagon had its door open, and Jessie stepped right in, rapping sharply on the wall as she entered.

"Yes?" responded an extremely oily voice.

"Are you the manager?"

"We're not responsible for any missing articles."

"I haven't lost anything."

"Oh?" A little of his excessive politeness fell away from his narrow, dark face. He had a long nose, slightly hooked, and dark, oiled hair that showed the toothmarks of a comb like grooves in obsidian. "What is it, then?"

"We're looking for work. My friend and myself."

"We're pulling out tomorrow."

"I know that."

"Well, we don't need anyone. Of course . . ." He looked Jessie up and down, his eyes widening as he studied her firm breasts, pleasantly curved hips, and beautifully molded face. "I guess we can always use another girl for the big show. We keep losing them anyway. Probably leave a couple behind here." The manager was practically talking to himself. "Your friend as good looking as you?"

"I'm not sure. Maybe he is," Jessie said with a touch of deviltry.

"A man?" He shook his head. "I've got all the roustabouts I can use. We're going to be a long while between shows now."

"He's a skilled man," Jessie said. "More than just a laborer."

"Oh? What's he do?"

Jessie told him. The manager frowned. "I'd have to see a demonstration, but look, Miss . . ."

"Columbine, Bessie Columbine."

"Yeah, well, look, Miss Columbine, there isn't going to be much money in this for a while. I don't have much lined up just now. We're drifting all the way to Mexico City. We're going to play before the Presidente. But just now things are tight. I don't even know if I can find accommodations."

"We have our own wagon."

"Share one, do you? Well, that's your business, I guess." He drummed his fingers on the desktop. "I'll take you. I want to see you in tights, girlie, I'll tell you that." The man was getting positively familiar. Jessie wasn't ready to discourage him yet. She gave a girlish titter.

"Then we're on, Mr. . . . pardon me, I didn't get your name either," Jessie said.

"Howell. Samuel Howell. Well, I'll tell you—you're on, girlie, but you got to understand it's no pay for the first month till we see how things work out, but you get all you can eat. Your friend I have to see, all right?"

"Fair enough."

40

Howell rose from his desk and oozed toward Jessie. He had nasty little ideas coming to life in his eyes. He rested a hand on her shoulder and let it slump slowly toward her breast. "Yes, I sure want to see you in tights, Bessie."

Jessie turned away with a bright smile. "You will, Mr. Howell. You sure will. Now I've got to get off to find my friend. He's gonna be real pleased!"

"Okay, yeah," Howell said, a little discouraged. "I always watch the big show. Come back around two, two-thirty, all right?"

"Yes sir. Two or two-thirty."

That suited Jessie fine; she wanted to see the big show as well. She was out the door and down the wooden steps before Howell could grab any more flesh. She passed a raging Chinese woman who was marching purposefully toward the manager's wagon. Some small conflict in the circus family, Jessie guessed.

Ki was at the ticket wagon.

"Is everything all right?" he asked.

"You have to audition."

"As what?"

"A knife thrower."

"Jessie . . ." Ki shook his head.

"I know," she said sympathetically, "but that's the way it has to be."

"To prostitute my art is shameful."

Ki was carrying it too far. "You'll survive," she told him playfully. He had the tickets, and they went on into the big tent with the rest of the crowd.

The ringmaster was standing in the center of the ring, bellowing through a megaphone. Jessie and Ki got as close to the front as they could, the third-row bench on the center aisle, and settled in to wait.

The show opened with the blare of trumpets. From the

side entrance the parade entered: girls in silver and pink tights; elephants wearing violet and gilt; tumblers turning handsprings; bareback riders; clowns; the strongman, a massive brute with a square, low forehead and arms the size an ordinary man's thighs.

Ki watched stoically, Jessie with a little more excitement. The trapeze artists had begun their ascent—John Quayle and a woman whom Jessie took for his sister. They went up the rope hand over hand, mounted a small platform, and waved to the crowd. The ringmaster directed attention to the trapeze, and Quayle began his show.

Jessie was lost in it. Quayle was incredibly strong, amazingly quick. Hanging by his knees, he caught his sister, who tumbled through the air toward him. Later he did a double somersault from one trapeze to the other, bringing the crowd to its feet.

Ki's thoughts were on Quayle as well, and as he and Jessie glanced at one another, she read his mind. Yes, she thought, he is a superb athlete, and very strong, obviously, but that doesn't meant he's the Death Angel. It must have taken years to develop the trapeze skills John Quayle displayed. It was more than simply a cover. The man was an artist at his work.

Ki's eyes weren't accusing, but they were thoughtful. Quayle bothered him. The man showed up at strange times, giving odd reasons for his appearance. He was always nearby when there was violence.

The elephants were putting on a show. There were eight of them, the youngest only shoulder-high. They sat up in unison, ran in a circle, trumpeted. One of them walked on a huge wooden ball.

The show ran on. All around Ki, people were applauding, children crying or yelling with glee, stuffing their faces with candy apples. Clowns began to cavort up and down the aisle, throwing buckets of water on each other, racing to and from a fire in the ring, where they pretended to put it out with bizarre equipment.

Ki saw that Quayle had finished his act and was gone. The elephants were being led out. A young woman in sequins was doing some amazing work on a white horse. The clowns rushed down the aisle in a mad scramble, honking horns, squirting each other, racing through the crowd to the shrieks of women and children.

A tall clown in a red and white harlequin costume was being chased by a short one with a huge false ears. He carried a rubber ax.

They charged up and down the aisle, then past Ki and Jessie. It was only instinct that saved Ki. He saw the clown face, white, expressionless, then the flash of steel, and he drew back, feeling the razor-edged knife score his abdomen before he could block it.

Ki kicked backward from the bench and rose in a crouch. People shoved him and laughed as the clown raced away. Ki's eyes followed the tall one in the harlequin outfit. His hand was pressed to his stomach.

"What is it?" Jessie asked.

Ki pulled his hand away and showed her the blood.

"Bad?" she asked with concern.

He shook his head. "No, not bad." But it could have been. Another half-inch, and the knife blade would have opened his bowels. There was no getting around it; the enemy knew they were there. The enemy meant to kill them before they could interfere.

They walked down to the stream behind the wagon encampment, and Jessie wrapped a strip torn from Ki's shirt around his abdomen for a bandage. This despite Ki's protests that it was nothing, hardly worth concerning oneself with.

"'Nothing' doesn't keep on bleeding," Jessie said. "We

can't have you dripping blood all over the place when you show Mr. Howell what you can do."

"Howell?"

"He's the circus manager, and we have a date with him."

"Jessie . . ."

"It's the only way."

"I'll have to go into town, then, and bring the wagon out. It has all of my material." Material that was never intended for show. But Jessie was right, this was not the time to be concerned with the purity of art.

"We have about forty-five minutes."

"Time enough," Ki said, buttoning his shirt, which was stained with blood. "Jessie—please be careful. This time it was me he slashed at. The next time it might be you."

"I knew that coming in, Ki."

"Yes, but be careful," Ki said again, and then he turned and walked away, heading north toward town.

Jessie started off toward the wagons beyond the trees. It didn't take much effort to find John Quayle's quarters. The wagon was bright blue, with the name QUAYLES in gold lettering. There was some business about "flying legends . . . amazing . . . stupendous . . ." painted below that.

Jessie hesitated on the steps without really knowing why. She looked at the wagon again and went on up. She had to know, one way or the other.

She tapped on the door and heard a stirring within, and then the door opened. John Quayle stood there shirtless, his muscles bulging, his eyes glowing softly.

"Miss Starbuck!"

"Hello, John. Busy?"

"Just changing. Come in."

He stepped back, and Jessie started up the stairs. Inside the door she hesitated. "Is your sister here?"

Quayle smiled, taking the question for shyness. "No.

She went down to the creek with the Taylor twins for a bath. They're with the tumblers, the Taylor twins, that is," John Quayle said, moving closer, resting his hand on Jessie's arm.

"Are they?" Her face was turned up to his, and as his mouth lowered to hers, Jessie's lips parted and Quayle kissed her hard, taking her into his arms, pressing his body against hers. Jessie's hands reached behind Quayle and gripped his hard-muscled buttocks, drawing him nearer. She could feel the swelling between his legs, feel the eagerness of his kiss. His lips traveled across her throat and down toward her breasts, his fingers undoing the first few buttons of her blouse.

"We're right in the doorway," Jessie said.

"So come in. Close the door," Quayle said logically.

"Your sister will be back soon."

"So lock the door."

"And I've got an appointment with Mr. Howell."

"Howell?" Quayle quit nuzzling her and stepped back, frowning. "What for?"

"I'm going with you. My friend Ki and I are joining the circus. Mr. Howell is going to give us a job."

"You?" Quayle held Jessie's shoulders. He frowned in puzzlement. "Why would you? You're not circus people."

"You don't want me along?"

"God, woman, what could I want more?" Quayle said with a laugh. "But I don't understand it, that's all."

"Well, we have our own reasons."

"The law?" he asked confidentially.

"Our own reasons," Jessie said in a way that allowed Quayle to believe he had guessed right.

"Terrific," he said. "I'm happy. What could I want more than to have you with us?"

"John, I'm traveling under a different name," she told

45

him. "I'm calling myself Bessie Columbine."

"Columbine." He smiled. "A lovely flower."

"Yes. You'll try to remember to call me that in front of other people, won't you?"

"If you want." He stepped to her again, and gathered her in his arms, kissing her. "But I plan to keep you away from other people as much as possible."

"Pardon me!" The voice was harsh and strident. Quayle stepped back as a woman with damp blond hair, a robe wrapped around her, squeezed into the wagon. "Don't let me disturb you, John," she said acidly. Apparently they didn't get along well.

"This is my sister Dorothy," Quayle said. "Dorothy, this is . . . Bessie Columbine."

"Good. Hello. Goodbye," Dorothy Quayle said. "I have to dress now, and I can't do it while you two are undressing."

"My sister has a peculiar sense of humor," John said with a shrug.

"I had to be going anyway," Jessie said. She looked to Dorothy Quayle, who was sitting on a wooden chair, rubbing her hair vigorously with a towel.

"I'll see you later," Quayle whispered. It was half a question. Jessie nodded.

"Yes. Later." Then she turned and went out into the hot sunshine, hearing voices rise inside the wagon as brother and sister wrangled. She would have to ask Ki if he was *sure* that the Death Angel was a man.

Chapter 5

Ki placed his equipment on the table. Howell stood nearby, arms folded, a cigar stuck in his face. At his shoulder was a big, bald, potbellied man named Schupe. He was some sort of factotum or assistant to Howell. The Teutonic name gave Jessie reason to look at him twice. The cartel had its international headquarters in Prussia. But Schupe was hardly menacing in that way, although his eyes enjoyed Jessie deeply.

"What the hell is all that paraphernalia?" Schupe asked.

His stubby, white little fingers reached out and handled the assortment of star-shaped, razor-edged *shuriken* lying on the table. Ki hissed softly in displeasure.

"Throwing knives," Jessie put in quickly.

"Never seen nothing like them."

"What's that other thing?" Howell wanted to know. "I've seen knife-throwers, but I've never seen anyone use something like that."

"*Sai,*" Ki said, watching as the circus manager picked

47

up the eighteen-inch-long, shining, trident-like weapon.

"Can't throw something like that," Howell pronounced.

"Point ain't even sharp," Schupe added.

"It isn't for throwing," Ki answered. "But it can be thrown. All cutting weapons can be thrown. All are harder than the human body."

"Than what?"

"Or the targets," Jessie put in.

"Yes." Ki was sulking again. He turned his back on the circus people. He had six throwing knives in his hands. Knives with the weight at the spade-pointed tips. They were thrown without a spin, the blade designed to fly true like a dart. Ki's knives had handles decorated with red tassels. He turned and bowed to Howell and then faced the target— the rough silhouette of a man painted on a flat board thirty feet away.

Howell was lighting a cigar when Ki began his moves. His right hand lifted, holding a shimmering piece of steel. The hand arced down and was filled again before Howell could blink. He saw only the red tassels, crimson blurs in the air, and heard the *thunk* of steel meeting wood. All of it was over in less time than it had taken Howell to light his cigar, the knives still quivering, outlining the figure of the man, two beside his head, one at the crotch, the others along the legs and torso.

"Jesus," Howell said appreciatively. "I've seen some knife work, but nothing like that!"

"Don't have any flair to it," Schupe said.

"What?"

"No razzle-dazzle."

"Jesus, that's the best knife work I ever saw in fifteen years of circus managing." Howell shook his head in admiration. "Fast. You see that speed?"

"Too damn fast," Schupe said. "That's the point, you

see. What kind of show is that? Audience don't see any more than you did. Whomp, whomp, it's all over."

Ki glanced at Schupe, then looked peadingly at Jessie. Didn't she realize that he was actually compromising himself here, informing any enemy operative that he was a martial arts expert?

Even as he was thinking that, Jessie gave him a look that said, "I know. I'm sorry, but we have to become a part of this."

"I think I get you," Howell was saying. "It's *too* good. We need some showmanship. Say, how about the girl as a target? Bessie?"

"No," Ki said sharply, surprising even Jessie. "I will not use a human target for the entertainment of others."

"It's the way it's done," Schupe said, spreading his hands. "All the best ones use a woman for a target."

"They cheat," Ki said. "I have seen such tricks. The knives sometimes come from the *back* of the board."

"Well, you can cheat too. No one can follow what you do, as fast as you are."

"I will not make cheap trickery of my art."

"Then do it straight!" Howell said with a huge grin. "The girl don't care, do you, Bessie?"

"I don't mind," Jessie said. "You won't miss, Ki."

"It's a foolish risk," Ki said stubbornly.

"Nonsense," Jessie said cheerfully. She was going to give them what they wanted. She had no doubts about Ki's skills, nor, she thought, did he. It was a matter of principle with him, that was all.

She walked across the narrow platform and placed herself against the painted figure, arms uplifted.

Ki grumbled a little as he picked up the seven *shuriken* on the table. Jessie stood smiling brightly, making a show of it, acting as if it were a real performance. That, Ki supposed, was the way to do it if they meant to hire on. So, as much as it galled him, he bowed to the empty tent, flourished an arm toward Jessie, and then flipped the first *shuriken* underhanded toward her. The pointed star imbedded itself in the wood, inches from her head. Ki bowed to the nonexistent audience, slowing himself deliberately.

When he was finished with his throws, some overhand, one from behind his back, he bowed again and Jessie came forward to take his hand and repeat the bow.

Howell was enthusiastic. "Well?"

"It's good," Schupe said, though he had enough of an accent to make the word sound like "goot."

"By God, I'm tempted to put them on salary," Howell said, slicking back his heavily pomaded hair.

"Wait and see. Wait and see," counseled Schupe, who seemed more an adviser than an assistant.

"Well, if you give me a show that good at Plainview— that's our first stop—I'll put you on salary. Work up a costume, will you?" he asked Ki.

"Yes sir," Ki said without inflection, bowing so that his chin dropped no more than half an inch. Then Howell and Schupe were gone, talking about the jugglers as they walked out of the tent.

"Pleased?" Ki asked, plucking his throwing stars from the board.

"Yes. Now we're free to get to work. The first thing we need to do is find those weapons, Ki."

"And then what? If we find them and stop the shipment, as you say, there will just be more arms delivered from another point. We obviously have to go to this Cheney's stronghold—wherever that is—but if they have a hundred men, I don't see what we can accomplish, Jessie."

"We'll do what we can. Meanwhile, I'm going to get a wire off to the United States marshal's office and see if we

50

can get some help. Maybe the Starbuck name still carries enough weight for someone to believe this is no joke."

"You are going back into town?"

"Yes."

Ki was concerned. "Be careful, please. Someone knows we are here, and will kill us if possible."

"I'll be careful. Stay out of trouble yourself, Ki."

"I hope to. But I must start looking for those weapons." He looked around the tent they were in, thinking how many places of concealment there were in a show this size.

After Jessie had gone and he had packed his blades away in the wagon, Ki got to looking around, and he started to think they weren't going to find anything at all. Some of the tents had wooden floors. Anything could be beneath them. The performers lived in wagons, any of which could be carrying contraband. There were rolling animal cages and the calliope, all the equipment used in the acts, all the crates the equipment was packed away in.

Nevertheless, he started. He started at one end, and was determined to work his way on through. The starting place was Howell's wagon, although it seemed one of the least likely hiding places.

Howell—was he a dupe or a revolutionary? There was no telling, although Ki would have guessed the former. And Schupe? He was just a little too unprepossessing, to Ki's mind. Too innocent. Too unlikely.

Ki waited in the shade beside the Howell wagon, listening and watching. There were two roustabouts having lunch near the wagon. After what seemed an interminable period they stretched and wandered off.

Ki slipped into the wagon.

He rifled the desk first, quickly, efficiently, looking for papers, letters, anything that did not have to do with the circus. He found nothing.

51

He felt beneath the desk, removed the drawers, checked the wall paneling. There was nothing at all. Perhaps underneath the wagon—much could be hidden under a false floor.

Ki had started toward the door with that idea in mind, when a glint of silver caught his eye. It gleamed in the crack between two floorboards, caught by a stray beam of sunlight through the high wagon window. Frowning, Ki got to one knee, glancing at the wagon door.

Unsheathing the curve-bladed *tanto* knife in his waistband, he pried at the tiny bit of metal. It came up easily and Ki, crouched there, turned it around in his fingers. It was a German fifty-mark piece. And it had no business being there. Not unless Howell entertained foreign visitors.

Ki pocketed the coin and rose quickly, hearing approaching voices.

". . .feed those big cats once we're out of sight of town."

"I'll see that we have a few cattle along."

"You'd better do something, Earl, or they'll be nibbling on *us*." That was Howell's voice, and Ki pulled himself back to stand beside the door. He waited, stilling his breath, but Howell did not come in. After a long minute Ki cautiously opened the door, but saw no one. He slipped out and was down the steps in no time, walking swiftly toward the crowded midway.

He went into the first tent he saw, intent on continuing his search. The sign outside said CHINESE MAGIC, but Ki hadn't been paying much attention. He found himself in a dusky tent with twenty other people, and on the stage was the Chinese woman.

Ki smiled and went forward to sit and watch.

"All secrets of the Orient, the mystical land of the East," the woman chanted in a charming singsong. "You must not think I use a trickery. I use the art of the sages."

52

She pulled a handful of glass balls out of the air and cast them down, and they turned into clouds of smoke. From the flaring golden sleeves of her silk costume she pulled a live hare, which was transformed with a wave of the wand into twin white doves.

There was a good response from the audience, a hearty round of applause.

"And now, Chan Li need a volunteer person," she said.

A farmer to Ki's left started to rise, but he was far too slow. Ki was already halfway to the stage, and he stepped up on it as the woman's eyes narrowed and the audience clapped some encouragement.

"What are you doing here!" the magician hissed in Chinese, through clenched teeth.

"Go away! I want someone else. I know your face. You can't fool me. Peeping person."

The audience was getting restless. Chan Li bowed and smiled. "Go away!"

"You had better go on with your show," Ki said stubbornly.

"Ah!" She made a thoroughly disgusted face. "Japanese devil!" It was the deepest insult she could think of, apparently. She returned her attention to the crowd. "Now it is my pleasure to make this man disappear."

That would give her pleasure, Ki thought.

He was led to a black and gold box to one side of the stage. She opened the door and turned the box to show the audience that there was no secret compartment, which of course there had to be.

"You will not make this go badly," the woman warned him. "You step out when I tap, step in when I tap again."

"All right." Ki, towering over her, was looking down into her dark eyes, liking the way the lights played on her intricately braided blue-black hair, which was piled on her

53

head and held in place with tortoise-shell combs. Ki stepped inside the box. She closed the door and he stood there as she talked to the audience. The back panel slid open silently and Ki stepped out, confused momentarily by a mirror and a drape of black cloth. He stepped behind the mirror and waited.

The box was opened, the audience applauded, and the girl tapped. Ki stepped back into the box, and after a moment was presented to the audience, which was appreciative once more.

"Thank you," Chan Li said. "You may return to your seat, sir."

"Thank *you.*" Ki bowed and walked off—backstage instead of to his seat, and he could see the Chinese woman's eyes spark. She had to finish her show, however; she didn't really have time to waste on Ki just then.

He watched the rest of the show from the wings, among her trunks and props—which he gave a casual search. The lady didn't look like a gun runner, but then Ki wasn't sure what a gun runner should look like.

Her show finished with a brilliant reddish explosion, harmless but effective, and she rushed offstage while the smoke settled and the audience applauded.

"Now why don't you go, Japanese devil," she said breathlessly, slipping from her robe to stand small, perfectly formed, intriguing, before Ki.

"Are all the people of your land so rude?" Ki asked.

"To Japanese, yes. Japanese tyrants, Japanese warlords!"

"So, you are like that," Ki said. The woman was letting her heavy canvas curtain down by means of a rope.

"Like what?" she asked, turning on him.

"You judge all men alike, all whites, all Japanese..."

"All Japanese *are* alike!" The curtain was down and she got busy packing her crates. Mirrors, platforms, and all the large props were left on stage. There was still another performance to go. Her animals and birds, the devices that had to be placed back in her costume, she collected with Ki following her.

"I wanted to explain about this morning—why I was looking into your window."

"There is no need. All Japanese are crazy for sex."

"I was looking for a thief. A man who took my purse," Ki went on. It wasn't a good lie, but then he wasn't a particularly good liar.

"So!" She turned, hands on hips, tiny and lively in her dark costume. "Now you say I am a thief!"

"You misunderstand me. Perhaps deliberately," Ki said, stepping nearer to her. She made a tiny disparaging noise and moved away.

"I have no time to talk to you," she said.

"Then later. We can talk tonight."

"All Japanese are sex-crazy."

"I didn't say anything about sex, woman!"

"That is the way of Japanese men," she said, nodding vigorously. "They dare not speak directly of what is on their minds."

Ki sighed noisily. "Woman, you are remarkable. Even for a Chinese."

"Go away, go away," she said with small shooing motions, and Ki, grinding his teeth, started away. He halted halfway across the stage.

"Be home tonight. I wish to speak to you."

She didn't answer. She had her head deliberately turned away from Ki, and she sang a Chinese song as she worked, cleaning up the stage. Ki ground his teeth a little more and left.

It was nearly sundown when he met Jessie at the wagon. She had bathed somewhere, brushed her hair to a high gloss, and put on a clean white blouse.

55

"You did send the telegram?" Ki asked.

"Yes. Any luck here?"

Ki told her about the coin. "Then I searched two tents. Perhaps not thoroughly, but enough to convince me they were not the hiding places. Between shows, it became too obvious that I was looking around for something. I said I was looking for you."

"We'll have to work at night. And tonight is the night for it. Before everything is rolled up and packed up tight."

"You are right," Ki agreed. There was something in Jessie's eyes . . .

But then there was something in Ki's eyes that said there was more to be hoped for from this night's work than a clue to the missing arms.

"What was that?" Jessie asked, and both of them turned toward the door. Ki moved quickly to blow out the lantern hanging on the wall.

Then he moved to the door of the wagon and opened it. Nothing was there, no one. He stepped down and walked in a slow circle around the wagon.

"Well?" Jessie said from beside him.

"He was here. Someone was here." Ki showed her a faint footprint in the dust, nearly twice the size of his own.

"A big man," Jessie said. "Very big."

"A giant."

They looked up the midway. The skies were coloring now, deep orange and scarlet, and thin streamers of cloud were drifting in. There was no one near the wagon, no one who looked suspicious.

There was nothing to be done. You can't engage the enemy in battle if he isn't there; you can't plan against him if you don't know who he is.

"Let's find those weapons," Jessie said. "Whoever he is, I've got a feeling he won't be far from them."

"Jessie, there's still time to back away from this," Ki said with genuine concern.

"If we did, it would be the first time, wouldn't it?" She smiled in the twilight glow. "I thought we were past that— past you worrying about me."

"I will never be past that," Ki said quietly. Her hand was on his forearm, but now it fell away. Across the circus grounds the torches were being lighted. The crowd, the last crowd for the last show, was moving onto the lot. It was time.

"Let's find the bastard," Jessie said.

★

Chapter 6

Ki took the north end of the circus, Jessie the south. Now, while the last big show of the stand was playing to the people of Amarillo, was the time to conduct the search. Jessie moved cautiously toward the wagons along the creek, those where the performers lived. Frogs were croaking farther downstream in the cattails. She saw the wagon that read CHINESE MAGIC on the side, and smiled faintly. Ki had told her of his improbable experience with the woman magician.

A roar went up from the big tent, and figuring back to the show she had seen, Jessie reckoned that John Quayle and his sister had begun their trapeze act. Good. Jessie wanted to—needed to—look in the Quayles' wagon. If there was anyone she wanted to clear of suspicion, it was John Quayle.

It was quiet among the wagons. The children had been put to sleep, and their parents were working. Another yell went up from the big tent. A yell of delight—maybe John had done his double somersault. If so, Jessie was behind schedule.

She went through the trees, which whispered with the rising wind, slipped up to the wagon, tried the door, and found it open.

"One point for John," she thought. People who have something to conceal lock their doors.

She was inside now, feeling her way across the wagon, wondering if she could risk a light, wondering how she was going to see well enough to search without one. Her eyes slowly adjusted. The starlight through the high window was enough to get her started.

She ran a hand under the thin mattresses of their beds, went quickly through Dorothy Quayle's closet, and was just opening heavy wooden trunk that sat in a corner, when a voice from the doorway asked, "Find it?"

Jessie turned slowly, her hand going to her derringer. John Quayle stood there, outlined against the night. He had a white towel draped around his neck, a robe wrapped around his body.

"John, I—"

"I know," he said, stepping inside and closing the door behind him. "You're just snoopy."

"That's right, yes."

"Go ahead. Take your time. If you can't find something, just let me know." His tone of voice indicated that he really didn't care.

"Your sister..."

"Not coming. They're having a hen party to celebrate the last night. They always do." Quayle was nearer yet, and Jessie tensed. She wanted to pull away from him, to play it safe. She also liked the man. She wanted to be in his arms, to feel his hands roving over her body, his rising need pressing against her.

59

Quayle's hands took her shoulders and drew her near, and Jessie threw caution to the winds. He was tall and strong and the night was cool. His robe fell open. He wasn't wearing anything underneath.

He was damp from the stream where he had bathed, but his flesh was warm. Jessie kissed his chest and felt his lips on top of her head, felt his fingers drop to her blouse front and begin working there.

Her blouse opened and her full, soft breasts bobbed free. Quayle's mouth went to them, teasing the taut nipples, taking first one and then the other between his teeth.

Jessie sighed, deeply pleasured. Her hands dropped to her waist, undoing her own belt. Then her searching fingers found Quayle's erect, throbbing shaft, and she placed it against her belly, liking the warmth of it, the eager need.

"I'll lock the door," Quayle said a little hoarsely, and as he turned away to do that, Jessie slipped from her clothing. Quayle found her sitting on the edge of his bed, naked, and he got to his knees to ease in next to her, his lips roaming over her inner thighs, Jessie's fingers in his hair.

"Come on," she said, and her voice, too, was a little husky. Jessie rose, turned her splendid bottom to Quayle and bent over, and the acrobat eased up behind her. Jessie's hand reached back and found his erection, placing the head of it to her soft inner warmth. Quayle sighed and plunged it home.

Jessie cupped his sack and pressed that against her cleft, as if she would take it inside too. The length of him, thick and satisfying, stroked against her as she knelt, head bowed, one arm braced against the wall, feeling Quayle's trembling. He ground himself against her, thrusting his shaft home time and again.

Jessie's body responded eagerly, adapting itself to Quayle, softening, growing fluid and warm. A soft gush of pleasure shook her. Quayle, trying hard to hold back his own completion, was making a poor job of it. He bent forward, clutching at Jessie's pendant breasts, his entire body trembling, his legs shaking, until with a soft cry he gripped her hips fiercely with both hands, burying himself in her to the hilt.

Jessie held still for a long minute, letting his tremors fade away, then slowly she began to move against him again, her inner muscles working against his shaft like tiny, clutching fingers Quayle sighed and stiffened, swaying slowly against her.

Jessie drew away from him and Quayle grabbed at her; she smiled in the night and sagged back on the bed, drawing Quayle after her. Her legs went high into the air, and as Quayle settled himself again, her feet locked together behind his back, holding him in as she began to sway and pitch against him, to roll and undulate, her hips moving constantly, until Quayle lifted himself onto his toes, his lips and teeth hunting for Jessie's soft breasts, feeling her encouraging hands run down his spine to his ass, run beneath him to touch his shaft where he entered her. She whispered soft words into his ears, words of no meaning, and Quayle climaxed again, his entire body rushing to completion, trembling, aching as he released his need.

And Jessie lay there, her own breath quieting, her heart settling to a slow, steady beating, her hands caressing the hard body of the athlete. And she knew—she knew he was not the Death Angel. Ki would have told her she was foolish; perhaps so. But she coudln't feel this way toward a man who carried death within him.

"Well," Quayle whispered into her ear, "did you find what you were looking for?"

"Yes," Jessie said quietly. "I found it." She kissed his throat and snuggled nearer.

Later she wasn't so sure that she had found what she had gone looking for. Later, in fact, she wasn't sure at all that

Quayle was what she wanted him to be, hoped he was. She found the knife while she was dressing.

Reaching for her boot, she felt the folded blanket under the bed, and as she moved it slightly, she heard the scrape of steel against wood.

Quayle was across the room, pulling his trousers on. Jessie glanced that way and then felt beneath the blanket, finding honed steel.

"Find everything?" Quayle asked. He meant her clothes, of course, or did he? He kept asking that, almost as if he were taunting her. Or was imagination taking over again?

"Yes," she said, rising. She slipped into her skirt and then sat on the bed, tugging her boots on.

Quayle walked to her and bent and kissed the top of her head. "You ought to tell me what's up," he said.

"What do you mean?"

"Why, when I first saw you, you didn't intend to join the circus. Then for some unknown reason you did. Grown-ups don't generally run away with circuses."

"I have a highly developed sense of adventure," Jessie said.

"Yes, and the next thing I know you've snuck into my wagon at night. Now, Jessie, I'd like to flatter myself and say you were obviously waiting to make love to me, but I can't be quite that conceited."

"I did step inside—to wait for you."

"Sure. You know, we've got a dozen performers leaving the show because of our schedule. Howell's got us heading for Mexico with only a half dozen dates to play on the way. Funny time to join up."

"You're irresistible," Jessie said lightly, going to tiptoes to kiss his cheek. "I'd follow you anywhere."

"I'll bet. What about this Ki fellow? Does he feel the same way?" Quayle asked, and Jessie laughed.

"I don't think so."

"Why does he travel with you, anyway? What is he to you?"

"Just a friend."

"A very unique one. I saw him throwing those knives..."

Quayle fell silent. How, Jessie wondered, had John seen that? He hadn't been around, unless he was peering in through a tent flap.

"And why aren't you using your name? Bessie Columbine, indeed."

"I'm running away from a possessive husband—he used to ask too many questions."

"I'll bet," Quayle grumbled, "he didn't get very many answers."

"No." Jessie kissed him again. "He didn't."

Then she went out, leaving Quayle standing in the doorway of the wagon, watching her, bemused. Outside, the starry night was still. The river rambled past, softly hissing in its sandy bed. In the circle of wagons there were few lights. Here and there a lamp softly glowed. Once, a baby squawked a complaint of some sort and then fell silent.

Jessie walked through the sycamores, thoughtful and slightly troubled. She was still warm with the afterglow of lovemaking, content and relaxed, but nagging doubts pecked at her consciousness. For all she knew, it could be Quayle who was the enemy. That knife—true, anyone could own a knife, but what was it doing under the bed? Was it the one that had cut Ki?

She stopped, sighed, and looked skyward. The moon was rising, huge and golden, segmented by the upper branches of the sycamores.

The shadowy figure detached itself from the surrounding darkness and lunged at Jessie. She saw the knife glint in the starlight, and reached for her pistol as she stepped back, already knowing it was too late. Her heel struck a tree root and she fell, the derringer flying free.

The second figure was twice the size of the first—a dark mountain blotting out the sky. Too large for a man, it had to be a bear. It grabbed the man with the knife and flung him aside. Jessie was sitting on the ground staring in amazement.

"You—all right?" the thing asked in a low, guttural voice.

"I think so."

Massive hands encircled her waist and put her on her feet as if she were a doll. He handed her the derringer, which she tucked away behind her belt. Looking at the man before her, she knew that the little double-barreled pistol she carried would be of no use whatsoever against a creature like him.

"Who are you?" Jessie asked.

The hulking thing answered with slow shyness. "I am Waldo."

"The strong man."

"I am Waldo," he repeated in a dull, deep voice. "Someone wanted to hurt you."

"Did you see who it was?"

"I didn't want them to hurt you," Waldo said, his slow voice sorting out the words, which seemed difficult for him.

"You've been following me," Jessie said with sudden knowledge. The footprints outside her wagon had to have belonged to this hulk.

"Yes." He looked at the ground, like an embarrassed schoolboy. A three-hundred-pound schoolboy.

"Why?" Jessie asked.

He answered frankly. "To see you. I like to look at you, and so I followed you around. Someone tried to hurt you."

Waldo wasn't one of the world's great conversationalists,

apparently. Still, if it hadn't been for the strongman's intervention, she would have been dead, and she knew it.

"Thank you for helping me," Jessie said. Waldo was silent, scuffing his toe against the ground. "Would you like to walk me back to my wagon?"

The man looked up like a grateful dog, a huge fluffy thing that didn't know its own strength. He nodded once, his eyes shuttling away.

"Good. Then I won't have to worry, will I?" Jessie said brightly, and she took his arm, massive, swollen with muscle. "Shall we go?"

The giant descended from being inarticulate to being struck dumb as Jessie hooked her arm around his and led him back toward the circus proper. Her head was not even near to his shoulder. He had a chest that must have measured seventy inches around. He was a freak of nature, a throwback to an earlier time, a gentle giant placed on the earth, destined to live a life he only half understood.

He puffed up as they walked the midway, Jessie like a child on his arm.

Jessie's mind was busy as they walked. *Who?* Who had tried to kill her tonight? John Quayle? Had he time? She didn't think so. Howell? Schupe? The Death Angel— whoever he was?

Ki was at the wagon, sitting on the wooden steps. He glanced up with ill-concealed surprise.

"So. You have found our footprint-maker."

"Yes."

"What happened?" Ki asked. Jessie patted Waldo's arm and released it.

"Someone tried to kill me. A knife."

"A man? A woman? Large or small?"

"The knife was large," Jessie said. "That's all I can tell you except that whoever it was, Waldo was bigger."

"That takes in a lot of people," Ki said. "He helped you?"

"Yes."

"For that I thank you, big man," Ki said, rising to bow toward Waldo. The giant blinked sleepily and answered slowly.

"They can't hurt her. I like to see her."

Ki and Jessie exchanged a glance. "Thank you," she said again. "Now we must say good night."

"I will sleep out here."

"It's not necessary."

"I will watch so that no one hurts you," Waldo said.

"Not tonight. I'll be all right tonight."

It took some time to convince the strongman, but eventually he ambled off, moving ponderously, his jaw clamped tightly. "Poor Waldo," Ki said.

"Yes, and poor me if he hadn't been there."

"You found nothing?" Ki asked.

"No. And you?"

"Nothing at all. And in the morning we move out."

"In the morning the circus moves out," Ki answered. "It doesn't mean we have to go."

"We have to go, Ki. You know it."

"Yes." He shook his head. "I don't like this, though, Jessie. I feel the evil hanging over us. I sense the bloodlust of someone. Twice he has tried already. He will not continue to fail."

"You're thinking about me again, not of yourself."

Ki shrugged. "I can't always be with you. Waldo won't always be near."

"No," Jessie told him. "We have to stop this man, Ki. He will kill and kill again. We have to stop Cheney and Cruz—they will kill hundreds, thousands if they have to, if they can. We have to stop the cartel. They have killed.

Many times. They have killed my parents. We can't back away from trouble."

"No." Ki hated it when she was logical. All that she said was true; it was just that he could not stand the thought of her being hurt. "We will do what we must. I will not mention retreat again."

Around them the circus quieted and went dark. The people of Amarillo drifted away in small groups. Children complained sleepily.

The show was over. The war was just beginning.

Chapter 7

Everyone was up with the dawn. There were no silk cos-
tumes in evidence, just work clothes, rough denims and
cotton shirts. The circus was moving and everyone was
expected to work, man and beast.

Elephants were tethered to the guy lines as the tents were
lowered. Parade horses were used to pack away canvas and
drag tent poles. Midgets and ticket sellers worked beside
the women who had been "Dancing Ladies of Arabia" the
night before.

Jessie and Ki helped load the wooden benches from the
big tent. The planks were broken into sections, the supporting iron frames loaded onto a wagon. A dozen people
were at the project, moving quickly, with practiced skills.

Ki and Jessie kept their eyes moving as they unfastened
the benches from their moorings and carried the planks to
the wagon.. Everything was in motion; they saw nothing
out of the ordinary. The weapons were hidden well, if they
were hidden here at all.

Jessie hadn't seen John Quayle that morning. The strongman had been there, watching, his mouth hanging slightly open. The strongman and later the Chinese woman.

Jessie had seen her walk past, tiny and elegant. Ki had lifted his hand and started to speak to her, but the Chinese woman had made a little "hmmph" sound and kept on walking.

"What was that about?" Jessie asked.

"Nothing. A Chinese female," Ki said, as if that explained something.

"A friend?"

Ki shrugged and gave his mouth a wry twist.

"You mean she doesn't care for you?" Jessie teased.

"Who knows what she cares for? The woman is a fanatic."

"I see," Jessie said, and Ki looked at her with suffering eyes.

"I know you're only trying to make fun, Jessie, but it isn't funny to me."

"All right."

"So please say nothing else."

Jessie wiped her forehead with the back of her hand and replaced her hat. "All right. I won't."

"And please," Ki said, "don't smile."

Jessie had several remarks she could have made, but Ki looked so serious that she held herself back, turning her face away from him so that he wouldn't see her smile.

The job seemed tremendous, but the circus people had done it many times, and by ten o'clock the circus was packed up, rolled away, stacked, and battened, ready to roll. Nothing remained of the midway but a few pieces of newspaper, some empty bottles, scattered straw, and a hard-packed section of earth that the rains and new grass would erase.

"Ready?" Howell asked, looking up to Ki, who sat beside

Jessie, their wagon near the back of the colorful column that was prepared to strike out southward, westward, toward the broad plains where the Comanche rode, toward the vast, empty New Mexico Territory, where revolutionaries planned their secret wars, toward the wilderness where hardly a man had walked, let alone a hulking, swaying pachyderm.

"Yes," Ki said, "we're ready."

"So am I. Amarillo be damned!" Howell turned his white horse toward the front of the column and removed his white hat, swinging it in a great circle over his head. They heard him shout, "Let's move, people! There's a fortune waiting for us in Mexico City!"

The wagons started on. The circus train, bright and glittering against the dry plains, moved out southward, in its wake elephants and camels, horses and dogs. Amarillo fell away behind them, and they were out on the broad and empty land.

"I like this less as we go along," Ki said, holding the reins of his two-horse team loosely in his hands, squinting at the sunny horizon.

"We haven't done real well. But there's a long way to go," Jessie answered.

"If possible, I would like to locate the guns before Plainview. That's our next stop, isn't it?"

"It is, but I wouldn't hope for a quick solution. A man prowling around out here is going to be much more noticeable than when the show's set up."

"Perhaps the law in Plainview is more cooperative than our friend, Marshal Caffiter."

"Maybe. We'll have to play that by ear," Jessie said. She had her hat off, letting it hang down her back by its thong. The wind ran soft fingers through her hair.

"We have to find out who the enemy is," she said after a time. "This blind man's bluff is no good."

"The man with the knife."

"Yes. Was it the same one both times? Or did one of them try to slash you, and another one come after me?"

"Jessie—" Ki hesitated. "This knife you found at Quayle's . . ."

"Yes, I know," she answered with a sigh. "I have to consider that. I'm not foolish enough to ignore it."

"Even though you don't feel he is guilty."

"My feelings don't count," she said, a little harshly. She asked again a question that had been on her mind. There was no real substance behind the question, but for some reason it nagged her.

"Could the Death Angel be a woman?"

Ki shrugged. "I don't know. I know no one who has actually seen him—or her. In fact, until now I half thought the Death Angel was a myth, not a real person at all."

"Just wondering," she said. The wagon slowed as they dipped down into a narrow, shallow wash and climbed up the far side, the horses straining in harness, leather creaking, the wooden wagon squeaking as Ki guided it up onto the flats.

"What woman did you have in mind?"

"I don't know. I don't even know what makes me suspicious. Perhaps I smelled something without realizing it. The scent of powder or perfume."

Ki shook his head. "It is possible. Who fits such a role, Jessie?"

"Dorothy Quayle?"

"I see."

"No, you don't see!" Jessie momentarily lost her temper. "She lives in that wagon, doesn't she? She could own the knife as well as John."

"That would clear John Quayle," Ki said, his voice carefully devoid of inflection.

"Stop it, Ki. I'm just suggesting it. It doesn't hurt to talk about it a little, does it?"

"Not at all."

"She is an acrobat, a trapeze artist. I'll bet she's got more strength in her shoulders and arms than a lot of men."

"Yes, Jessie."

"You're impossible today. All right," Jessie said, "another woman. How about Miss Chan Li?"

"If you're trying to annoy me, Jessie, it's useless."

"Annoy you? I'm just throwing her name out. Why not Miss Chan Li for a female Death Angel."

"Too small."

"Too small? What has size got to do with it? We've seen some small people handle weapons before."

"What reason have you for even suggesting this?" Ki asked. "She's only a showgirl. A magician. An entertainer."

"She's Oriental."

"Ah, I see—and therefore suspect."

"Therefore it's possible she knows the martial arts."

"I cannot accept that," Ki said. "No. We are searching for a man."

"Probably. But with a myth..."

Jessie fell silent for a long while, rocking and swaying with the movement of the wagon, its motion strangely reminiscent of another sort of movement. She found herself thinking of John Quayle, of his strong, plunging body, and hoping against hope that he wasn't the man they wanted.

There was supposed to be a large pond ten miles to the south, and they were counting on it for the animals. It turned out to be fifteen miles, and when they found it, it was half mud. Howell was having a temper tantrum and Jessie didn't blame him. She passed the lions and tigers prowling their cages, sick with the motion and the heat of the day, mad for water. If they weren't watered regularly, they would be very tough to handle. The elephants trumpeted to the crimson and purple skies.

"We can't go on. We'll have to make do."

"There's not enough water," Schupe said.

Howell turned on him. "Damn you, I know that! But we don't have any promise we can find water ahead. It's near dark. Ben," he said to the elephant handler, "tell Verdugo to water his big cats first, then the bear, then your beasts— try to hold them back a little if you can."

Ben looked doubtful. It probably wasn't easy to hold back an elephant that wanted water. "Then the horses," Howell said. He looked very upset.

"This is only the first day," Ki said at Jessie's shoulder. "And how many will we be on the road? How far is it to Mexico? How many miles will be dry ones?"

It didn't make any sense, if everything was on the up and up. Even if the Mexican Presidente were offering a million pesos for a show, a sane man would have turned him down. The dry days, the hot sun, the empty land— empty but for those Comanches who were out here somewhere. No, Howell had either gotten too greedy or been forced into something that was not quite sane—like smuggling weapons to revolutionaries.

Jessie and Ki kept their wagon a little separated from the others, but it wasn't going to be possible to have much privacy from here on. Their movements were going to be easily observable.

There were a half-dozen campfires going, with men and women clustered around common pots, when Jessie went walking. Walking slowly through the camp, just watching. Where were the weapons? Who was guarding them?

It was an odd and eerie night. Dark skies with clusters of silver stars, the red, flickering campfires, the sounds of exotic animals.

The big man was behind Jessie, but then she was getting used to it. Up to a point it didn't matter.

"Hello." John Quayle was in blue jeans and a white shirt. He came up to Jessie, gathered her in his arms, and swung her around, kissing her throat.

"Careful. My bodyguard."

Quayle glanced across her shoulder. "I can't think of a better job," he said. "I'd like to guard your body, Jessie— Bessie, damn you, mysterious women. How did you come to pick up Waldo, though?"

They walked away from the camp, the stars growing brighter as the firelight dimmed. Jessie told John about the knifing attempt, listening, watching, trying to sense whether he knew anything about it.

If he did, he was a very good actor. He took Jessie by the shoulders, looked down into her eyes, and said, "That scares me. That really does. I'm glad Waldo has adopted you. I feel like sticking close myself."

"Maybe they thought I was someone else," Jessie said.

"Maybe. If you'd tell me what you're doing with the circus, maybe we could figure it out together. Maybe I know something that could help."

"I can't tell you."

"Well, then . . ." Quayle shrugged. He kissed Jessie full on the mouth, feeling her slack against him, her pelvis touching his, moving with the slightest pressure.

"He's still there," she said.

"Who? Waldo? Well, damn him—go away, Waldo?" Quayle said, raising his voice jokingly. "I mean enough's enough."

"John, your sister," Jessie began as they started walking back toward the wagons. "She—"

"Why talk about her?" Quayle said, and his voice had a sudden edge to it. He had been walking with his arm around her waist, and Jessie felt the sudden tensing of muscle, the unease.

"I just wanted to ask you something," she said with surprise.

"I don't think it's right to talk about her," Quayle said, and from his tone it was obvious that he meant he *wouldn't* talk about his sister.

Why? Jessie frowned in the darkness. "All right," she said quietly, but her mind was running through a thousand possibilities, wondering.

Waldo was still behind them when they got back to the wagon; something was going to have to be done about that. The giant had done her a favor, but she couldn't have him following her about. She wanted her privacy, and she needed the freedom of movement that life with Waldo just wasn't providing. The trouble was, talking to him seemed unlikely to have much effect. As far as intelligence went, Waldo's best recommendation was that he was *large*.

"I'll see if I can't get him to stop it," John Quayle said as he stood with one foot on the wagon steps, his hand resting on Jessie's hip. "Though in a way I like the idea."

"You won't like it when he's watching us enjoy play-time."

"No." Quayle smiled thinly. "I'll talk to him. You just watch out for yourself. If you won't tell me what the trouble is, what you want . . . well, then, be careful, Jessie. Please."

Ki was out when Jessie told John Quayle good night and went in. Just so she wouldn't be lonely, someone had dropped in to keep her company.

It was Schupe—round, smug, and pink. He was seated at the small half-moon table against the far wall. For an intruder, he looked awfully damned sure of himself. He was spinning something on the table, and as Jessie drew nearer she could make out what it was—a silver fifty-mark piece.

"Hello, Miss Columbine," the man said without rising. His accent had changed since Jessie spoke to him last. It had deepened and grown authoritative. He was smiling insufferably, deeply pleased with himself for some reason.

"I'll have to ask you to leave." Jessie tossed her hat onto the bunk. "I can't imagine why you think you have the right to come in here."

The silver coin clattered to a stop and Schupe covered it with his hand. "Why, do not allow yourself such excitement, Miss Columbine. I wanted to see that everything was all right with our new friends, with Mr.—what was his name? Never mind. With you and the Chinaman."

"He's Japanese and American," Jessie said, and realized that she had said the wrong thing. She didn't intend to give information away. Not to Schupe.

"So." Schupe lifted his chin toward the walls of the wagon, walls decorated with weapons old and new, many well baptized. "Your friend the knife-thrower is well provisioned."

"I wish you would go."

Schupe didn't move, and there really wasn't anything Jessie could do about it, short of drawing her pistol and forcing him out at gunpoint.

"Many weapons," Schupe said.

"A part of the act. He has many tricks."

"Yes." Schupe was momentarily thoughtful. "I would wager that he does, Miss Columbine."

The repetition of her assumed name, the peculiar emphasis he put on it, was starting to bother Jessie. She knew that it was probably intended to do just that, and she tried to ignore it. Schupe rose.

"I have been informed that you came to the office to see us and we were not there. What was it you wanted?"

"Nothing, I wasn't there."

Schupe was fingering the coin. He rose and ostentatiously pocketed it. He had gotten his story wrong. Apparently someone had seen Ki at the wagon, however; seen him and turned him in. By the time Schupe got the story, it was Jessie who had done it.

"No? No difference. I thought you needed something, that is all." He nodded to Jessie. "Good night, then, Miss Columbine. Anything at all you need—you tell me, yes?"

And then he was gone, leaving a bad taste in Jessie's mouth. What the hell was he up to? She didn't have to look far to convince herself that Schupe had been searching the place. Items were out of order. Ki was very habitual, very neat. So was Jessie. Someone who wasn't very neat had been through the trunks.

He had found the coin. What else had he found? While Jessie stood out front, talking to Quayle, the man had had plenty of time to rearrange things and seat himself at the table as if nothing were happening. But something *was* happening—the trouble was, Jessie was becoming less and less sure what it was, and the feeling of helplessness she was developing was disconcerting. Jessica might have had her failings, but being timid and helpless had never been one of them. She didn't like it, didn't like it a bit. There was no one to trust, no one at all but Ki. And what would she do without him?

And where the hell was he now?

Chapter 8

The panther prowled his cage, and with each step the wagon rocked slightly. The velvet paws rose and fell, and a motion like a slow pulsing swayed the rolling cage. Ki's hand searched the compartment hidden beneath the floor of the wagon. He scented axle grease and the acrid smell of the big cat, which paced and paced the miles of sage and chaparral. His hand found something in the narrow concealed compartment. It was cool, metallic, oil-smeared. He couldn't discover any more, but then he didn't need to.

The rifles were there. In the false floor of the big cats' cages. Perhaps there were other places of concealment, but some were definitely hidden there. Ki had luckily found a board that had rotted and then been broken free. The compartment was intended to be reached only through the interior of the panther's cage. A very secure arsenal indeed. The panther growled, its snarl chilling and primitive. Ki could do nothing more where he was, and so he slid out from under the wagon.

"You!"

Ki recoiled at the sound of the voice, went automatically into a fighting crouch, knees bent, hands raised to strike or defend. There was no need for either course of action.

It was the Chinese woman, and she stood in the darkness wearing a black silk suit, her hair loose, tapping a toe as she glared at Ki.

"I will report you now, Japanese devil. I will report you and they will send you back to Japan."

"Wait!" She had turned away, and Ki grabbed her arm to turn her back. She slapped his hand.

"Don't you touch me. What are you doing here, anyway? I think you are a sneaky bad man."

"I can explain it to you."

"Your purse is lost," she said with heavy mockery.

Ki sighed inaudibly. Rather than start a new lie, he continued with the old one; maybe, given time, she could accept the fantasy.

"Yes, I was looking for it."

"It would be gone, thrown away," the woman said.

"No. Listen—" Ki looked around. "We can't stand talking here." If someone wandered by and Chan Li told her story, Ki would be put in a very bad light. It just wasn't normal for people to lie under the big cats' cages at night.

"No. We cannot talk."

She started away and Ki fell in beside her, hooking her elbow with his fingers and thumb. She tried to snatch her arm away, but Ki kept his grip.

"Leave me alone."

"I have to explain this to you," he said.

"I explain! I explain to the boss. Mr. Howell should know."

"Know what? What was I doing?"

That seemed to stop her. "I don't know." She halted in her tracks. "Something bad."

"No. Merely something you don't understand. Anything

79

you don't understand, you think is bad. Like me. Like all Japanese."

"I understand you," she said sharply. "I understand Japanese."

"All right." Ki didn't want to start that debate up again. "But you don't understand what I was doing tonight. It was not bad at all."

"Maybe not." She seemed to have cooled down a little. "I go home now."

"May I walk along with you?"

She started to refuse automatically, but then she seemed to soften ever so slightly. She shrugged and started on, her arms folded so that each hand was in the opposite sleeve of her jacket. "I do not know what a man could do under a big panther's cage."

"I was looking for something," Ki admitted.

"Something stolen. Your purse."

"Yes," he said, regretting the necessity to lie.

"I don't think so. I think maybe you are a man who has come to make trouble for the circus."

"Why would you think that?"

They had veered away from the wagon camp a little, and now they were on top of a low knoll overgrown with dry grass. The stars were very bright. Down around the pond, frogs croaked incessantly in a loud chorus.

"I am not so stupid, Mr. Japanese."

"My name is Ki."

"So?" She shrugged again. She looked up now at Ki with star-bright dark eyes. "I have heard them say trouble might come to us."

"You heard *who* say this?"

"It is not important."

"Mr. Howell?" Ki asked.

"Mr. Howell maybe. And another man with him, maybe. They did not see me. It was at Amarillo, you see. I was

80

washing in the creek, you see? I heard the men coming and I hid in the trees. I heard everything they said."

"They said that there was trouble coming. Why?"

"Trouble to the circus. Maybe someone would try to stop them. That was what they said."

"They didn't say who?" Perhaps, after all, Howell knew who he and Jessie were.

"I did not hear them if they did. I was hiding quietly. They walked past. They said, 'Make sure those wagons are watched at all times.'"

"What wagons? The animal cages?"

"That is so," the woman sighed. "And so I see you, a Japanese, skulking around my wagon, watching the panther's cage. I think you are the one who has come to bring trouble to the circus."

"No," Ki said after a while. "I didn't bring it, but it's here. May I give you some advice? Don't go on with this show. When we get to Plainview, leave the circus. It'll never get to Mexico."

"Leave the circus? And do what? What do you think a Chinese girl can do in this country for work? I am a magician. If I do not do magic, then I am nothing."

"I don't want you hurt."

Ki had moved a step nearer, and the girl had moved half a step away. It was a progression that Ki liked. He took another step.

"I must turn you in," she said, and her voice caught a little as she said it.

"All right." Ki rested a hand on her waist.

"I cannot have someone ruin the circus. It is my home."

"I understand." His other hand went to her shoulder and remained there. He didn't have to take another step. The woman had another objection to make, but halfway through she seemed to forget what it was.

"I must . . ."

Ki took advantage of the pause to place his lips to hers, to taste her sweet lips and feel the involuntary slackening of her body, the small trembling.

"Bad," she said, only her voice was a taut whisper. Her hand rested on his chest. She stepped back, shaking her head. "You are so bad, Mr. Ki."

Then she turned and started away, hesitating once as if she would say something else, but she went on toward the camp, and the night swallowed up her small dark figure. Ki looked to the skies and took a deep, slow breath. Then he started back toward the encampment. He still had a night's work to do.

With the dawn they were rolling southward, looking out across vast, dry, apparently endless plains, where there was nothing but dead grass and patches of nopal cactus, sometimes acres of the stuff, growing head-high, nearly impenetrable.

But there was no sign that a human being had ever tried to scratch a living from the sere and barren land. Ki drove the wagon. Jessie, lost in thought for much of the time, sat beside him. The wagons were all coated with dust now, dulling their garish colors. The elephants bawled constantly and the big cats roared their displeasure.

"This must have seemed to be a good idea," Ki commented once, "to have a circus smuggle guns. To hide the weapons in the floors of the wagons. But I wonder, can we even make it to New Mexico Territory? Water cannot be more plentiful, the way must be hard."

"The cartel is not going to worry about a few animals, Ki. Nor a few people. Once we're out of sight of Plainview, anything can happen."

"Yes." Ki nodded thoughtfully. It was true. If the animals had to be disposed of, then that would be done. If there were people in the way, then they too would have to go. There were a million square miles of territory at stake, a new nation in the planning, and nothing could be allowed to stand in the way of that plan.

"Have you thought exactly what this means?" Jessie commented. "If they somehow succeed, that is? A new nation between the United States and Mexico. A militaristic country run by a criminal dictatorship? There'd never be any security for the United States or for Mexico. California would be cut off—and maybe in time annexed, who knows?"

"It is a mad scheme," Ki said. "The United States will not allow it."

"And how are they going to stop it? Move the entire army to the Southwestern frontier? There's not a nation on this earth that hasn't belonged to different peoples at different times. The history of the world is the history of change through force of arms."

"Perhaps. I know this much—they are very serious about it. There are enough weapons to outfit an army."

"They have the army. Every bandit in the Southwest, all of Chato Cruz's people, dissatisfied Mexican peons, renegade Indians—everyone with a dream of his own. Of course, their personal dreams won't count, once things are settled militarily. The army of criminals that Cruz commands will be disbanded—one way or the other."

"Is that a settlement?" Ki stood in the wagon box. "It is, Jessie. Can you see it? Due south."

Jessie nodded. She could see Plainview now, rising up out of the plains. "And everything past that..."

"What?"

"Everything on the other side of that little town is another country."

"Not yet," Ki said, a little grimly. "They may think the deed has been done, but it hasn't."

83

"Thank you, Ki." She looked at him and touched his shoulder. "I think I need to hear that just now."

They arrived in Plainview at the hour before sunset. It was too late to set up for an evening show, and they didn't try. The wagons were circled on an empty field north of town, in the shelter of a row of young salt cedar trees. Kids from Plainview thronged to the field. They didn't have a whole lot to amuse themselves with out here, on the ragged edge of civilization, and the circus was the biggest moment of their lives.

Ki and Jessie headed for town as soon as things were settled. Plainview wasn't exactly a town: a few false-fronted buildings, a scattering of adobes, a general store at the crossroads, where the telegraph line ended. There was a saloon, of course, and some of the circus folk had already gravitated that way. Jessie went to the telegraph office, which was only a nook in the general store. A balding man wearing rubber sleeve guards and a green celluloid eyeshade sat reading a newspaper behind the counter.

"Help you?"

"I was hoping there'd be a wire for me."

"Name?"

"Starbuck."

"No wires for nobody," the man said, folding the paper. "Why'd you ask for my name?"

"One comes in, I'll know who to look for, won't I?" He had a voice and a face like dry parchment. "You a circus lady?"

"Yes."

"I'll let you know, then. How long you folks staying?"

"I'm not sure. Perhaps only one day."

"I got a boy . . . you got girlie dancers?" he asked, his eyes narrowing with some secret fantasy.

"They have some dancers, yes. If the wire comes in . . ."

"Where from?"

"If any wire comes in, please let me know immediately."

"Sure, all right," the telegrapher said, and got back to his paper.

"Can you tell me where to find the town marshal?"

"Sure. Quarter-mile south of town. Under a white wood cross." The telegrapher guffawed at his own joke. It didn't take much to amuse the little man.

"You have no marshal?" Ki asked.

"No live one. Say, what are you, a Chinaman?"

Ki didn't bother to answer. Together he and Jessie left. They stood on the boardwalk outside, staring toward the town, listening.

"There's no local law, and we can expect no help from the United States marshal's office."

"Why?" Jessie was exasperated. "They can't simply ignore this."

"They have."

"Do they think it's a joke?"

"It's just too large for them to believe, Jessie. And we," he added unhappily, "are now quite alone with this problem."

They were that, indeed. There was no one else to turn to.

The circus grounds were quiet when they got back. Most of the able-bodied men were in town seeing how quickly they could get drunk. John Quayle was nowhere to be seen. The Quayles' wagon, Jessie noticed, was as far from theirs as possible. Some of Dorothy's influence? What did the woman have against Jessie? Or was she one of those sisters who takes on the role of mother and doesn't know how to drop it?

Jessie was exhausted. Mentally exhausted. She was tired

of thinking about all this. She needed something she could get hold of and physically handle.

"I've got to get some sleep," she apologized.

"There is nothing else to be done. Tomorrow will be a busy day."

Ki himself didn't look ready to sleep. "What about you?" Jessie asked.

"I will take another look around the wagons."

"You think there are still more weapons hidden?"

"One never knows."

No, Jessie thought, One never does know. But she thought she did.

She was right. Ki went out again and Jessie, yawning, locked the door. He wouldn't be back until morning. She undressed and lay down to stare at the ceiling for a long while, a string of faces passing in procession through her mind. Friends, enemies, the guilty and the innocent. The game was to try to sort them out properly.

Ki rapped on the wagon door and it slowly opened. Not much, only an inch or two, enough for one dark eye to peer out.

"Yes? What is it?"

"It's Ki."

"Yes," she said again, "what is it?"

"Let me in, please."

"You have something for me?"

"Yes, I do," Ki said quietly.

Chan Li opened the door and stepped back. Ki noticed in the first few seconds that she was naked. And if the woman had been particularly observant, she would have noticed what it was that Ki had brought for her.

Ki locked the door behind him.

Chapter 9

"I was not expecting..." the Chinese woman backed away, reaching for her robe. The lamplight glossed her body, turning it to gold.

"Don't bother putting that on. You knew I would be coming."

"No, I did not." She hung her head. She had long legs for a Chinese. Her dark hair, hanging loose as it was now, dropped to her hips, flowing over her shoulders, partially concealing her small, firm, dark-nippled breasts. The patch of dark hair between her thighs was luxuriant, drawing Ki's eyes.

"You are very beautiful," Ki said. "Did you know that?" He moved nearer and stroked her shoulder. He smiled and slowly turned her, looking at her from behind, the drape of her hair, the sinuous line of her spine, the honey-colored buttocks, flaring, smooth.

"You flatter me because you want me."

"I do want you," Ki said. "But I tell you the truth."

"May I please undress you?" she asked. Her eyes were turned down and her hands clasped.

"Yes," Ki said. "You may do that."

Her fingers were nimble and quick. She removed his shirt, her breath coming quickly, interrupted by the small noises of concentration. Ki felt her hands resting on his muscular back, felt the moist touch of her lips.

Then she was in front of him, carefully folding his shirt. She placed it on the chair back and came to him again, bowing in adherence to some ancient, nearly forgotten custom.

Ki sat as she silently directed, and she removed his rope-soled slippers. She sat at his feet for a minute, rubbing them, her dark hair veiling her face.

"You will stand again?" she asked, and Ki complied.

Her dark eyes sparkled, and her mouth smiled thinly as her fingers undid Ki's belt and then the buttons of his fly.

His erect shaft came free and he heard her inhale sharply. She held down his trouser cuffs as he lifted his feet from his pants. She rose, carefully folding the trousers.

"Please," she said when she returned. She motioned toward her bed, which was a mat on the floor, covered with a quilted cloth.

Ki sat down, his legs crossed, and the woman sat facing him. Her hands reached out and cupped Ki's sack as he leaned forward to kiss her, his own fingers going to her crotch, sliding inside, finding her moist and soft.

"Yes, I like that. And the rising warrior," she said, her fingers running up and down Ki's erection, pausing to toy with the head of it, inflaming him further. Their lips met and the woman murmured with satisfaction as Ki kissed her, his fingers stroking her soft inner flesh. Her own hand worked more rapidly at Ki's shaft, manipulating it knowingly, her amazingly soft fingers playing with the cap, then running to the base of it to briefly, gently handle the pendant sack.

"Please," Chan Li said again and spread her legs, scooting forward until she was on Ki's lap and she had taken his shaft to her deep, tender cleft. She stroked herself with the head of Ki's member for a moment, her head thrown back, her lips slightly parted to reveal straight white teeth.

Then, with a lift and a thrust, she was on him, settling deeply as Ki reached behind her to help lift her, to hold her smooth, solid buttocks.

They sat facing each other, nibbling at lips and throat, ears and mouth as the woman swayed from side to side, Ki's fingers reaching around from behind to touch her where he entered her, to feel the liquid warmth of the woman.

Ki bowed his head and took a taut nipple into his mouth, rolling it between his lips, teasing it with his teeth. His legs straightened out beneath Chan Li and he lifted her higher yet, his body's rising need encouraging him to rock against her, to arch his back and sway.

There was intense concentration on her face. Her hands gripped Ki's shoulders, contracting spasmodically. Ki began to lose his own composure. He lifted himself higher yet, needing his completion. Together they toppled onto their sides, Chan Li's leg lifting higher into the air as Ki stroked against her, harder and deeper yet.

Her cry filled the air, deep, trilling, surprising. She bit at Ki's shoulder, threw her body against his, writhed and twisted as Ki held on, his own body driving itself toward a massive climax that he found moments later. He held her to him, his mouth pressed against hers, bruising her lips against her teeth, his arms locked around her, squeezing off her breath, as he felt his own urgent need slowly ebb away.

"And so," she whispered into his ear, "I was right about Japanese men. All sex."

"Sometimes," Ki answered, kissing her eyebrow.

"But I was wrong about you being a bad man."

"Yes. You were wrong."

"Good." She yawned and her eyes closed. "I am glad I was wrong."

And then she was asleep, and Ki lay there in the darkness, thinking. Thinking about something Jessie had said, perhaps not in earnest.

Could the Death Angel be a woman? Could this creature, soft and knowing, gentle and eager, be a killing thing? Why not? A tiger proves tender to its mate. A woman must have a man. Why not the Death Angel, if she were female?

He looked down into her sleeping face and shook his head. Preposterous. The idea was not sound. Still, it was a long while before Ki was able to finally fall asleep on that night.

Morning was bright and glaring. Jessie had risen with the dawn and gone out to look at the circus wagons, to study the birds winging across the tinted skies.

He wasn't there. Still not there. John Quayle hadn't been around for nearly twenty-four hours, and that seemed wrong. Last night could have been devoted to lovemaking, but John was absent. Why? And where?

Jessie shrugged it off and walked down to the Big Top area. The tent lay folded around the center pole. It was still early for work. They had set up a shower for the women, and it was being filled with buckets of water. Jessie took her turn in the bucket brigade and then showered with the harsh yellow soap. When she came out, Ki was nearby.

"Good morning," she said. Ki answered automatically. His thoughts seemed far away.

"Your man is here, I see," Ki commented.

Jessie looked around hopefully, but it was only Waldo—

hulking, guileless, annoying. "I'm getting tired of him," Jessie said, "but I can't get rid of him."

"Don't be so eager to chase the dog away. The wolves may be near."

"Platitudes, at this time of the morning?"

Ki grinned. "It expressed what I wished to say."

"Have you got your costume put together?" Jessie asked as they walked toward the wagon.

"Costume?" Then he recalled that Howell had wanted him to wear some sort of costume. "I don't know what to do about that. I don't care if he is satisfied or not."

"Oh, yes we do. We don't want to get ourselves fired now."

"No, you're right. Perhaps Chan Li has something—a large robe would do."

"Chan Li?"

"The woman," Ki said, making an awkward, nearly embarrassed gesture.

Jessie didn't respond. They had reached the wagon to find Howell there, waiting. "Listen," he said, "you've got the south tent. Three shows. Twelve, four, and eight. All right?"

"Yes," Jessie said.

"Okay. Make sure you're on time," Howell said. The manager was nervous; why, they couldn't guess. "I've got some of the boys painting a sign for you. Give the people the same show you gave me and Schupe, and everything will be all right."

"We'll try to please them," Ki said. His voice was a little stiff, but Howell didn't notice it. He wasn't used to dealing with people *as* people. They were cogs in his circus, that was all. The circus manager touched the brim of his derby hat and walked away, shouting at Ben, the elephant man.

"There has still been no answer to the telegram?" Ki asked.

"Not yet."

"Then we can expect none."

"I'm afraid not."

But they had passed the point where they were hoping for help. Ki went off toward Chan Li's wagon to try to borrow some sort of robe for the performance, and Jessie went inside.

She closed the door and sagged onto the bed with a sigh. She wasn't looking forward to being Ki's target for three performances, even though she had the greatest confidence in his skill.

"What," she wondered, "should I wear?"

She didn't have much with her, but there were a few dresses in the wagon's closets, among them a sheer white silk gown with pleated sleeves that fell open like cones. Maybe for this...

She was aware of the warmth before anything else. The warmth that was not human—how she knew that, Jessie couldn't have said, but she knew right away that it was not a human warmth. There was the warmth and then the drape of weight, the strength, the incredible flex and grip of primitive muscle.

The python dropped onto her shoulders and its body coiled around her. Its body was massive, amazingly strong. There was thirty feet of snake around her, an incredible weight of moving, crushing muscle.

Jessie froze, bracing herself against the heaviness of the thing.

Don't move, she told herself. *It has to realize you're too large for it to eat.*

She knew little about snakes, but she had learned that the python could eat a whole lamb if hungry enough. But kill a human to eat? To eat, no, but it was capable of killing. All too capable.

Jessie was pinned to the floor, half in and half out of the closet. The snake continued to cling to her, to writhe and coil, but it seemed indecisive, if such a word could apply to a creature with a brain the size of a walnut.

Jessie tried to reach for her gun, but one of the python's coils was tight around her waist, preventing her fingers from grasping the derringer behind her belt.

Anger and frustration overwhelmed her. She struggled wildly. It was a mistake. The python's coils tightened as she tried to release herself. The bands of muscular power wound around her breast and waist, her thighs. Moving, crushing, living, mindless thing, the python had begun to constrict.

The door to the wagon was opened without haste, and someone stepped in, then, with a cry, rushed across the room. Jessie looked up, seeing Ki only as a dark figure in the gray blur of perception.

"My eyes," she said.

"Just a minute. Hold on. I'll get him."

"I can't see you."

"It's all right, Jessie. It's the blood supply being cut off, that's all. I'll set it right."

"Ki...this is ridiculous." She tried to laugh, but she hadn't the breath for it. She was locked tightly in the big snake's coils, and she could feel it constricting more yet; she knew that in a minute her ribs would collapse, and respiration would be cut off completely. The reptile's all-too-efficient, primitive method of killing was being brought to bear.

"Ki..." She couldn't see what he was doing. He was near the snake's head.

"Just a minute, please!" Ki said, a bit frantically. How

the hell do you fight something like this! he wondered. The answer should have been simple, and it was, once it occurred to him.

The snake was a living thing, a vertebrate, made up of muscle and bone and blood vessels. It had a network of nerves that connected the body with the brain. The only problem was to locate them. Ki's hands worked near the python's head. The jewellike, lifeless eyes stared back at him. The tongue flickered out and tested Ki's flesh, wondering what it was.

Jessie looked bad—pale, unmoving. Ki found the bundle of nerves at the base of the python's skull and applied pressure with his fingertips. There was an immediate reaction, and Ki sighed with relief. He could feel the muscles relax, and as he increased the pressure, using the very same technique he would have used to apply a sleeper hold to a human being, the snake slowly went slack. Its nerves were paralyzed. Nothing was getting through from the tiny brain to the massive body.

"Jessie!"

She only moaned. Her eyelids flickered open, but there wasn't any consciousness in her green eyes. Ki reached over and slapped her face, his handprint appearing red against her bloodless cheek.

"Jessie!" he said again, sharply.

She was looking at him, and slowly her eyes began to focus. "What is it? Who is it?" she asked absently.

"Get up, Jessie."

"Time already?"

Ki was still applying pressure to the python's nerve cluster, but he had no great faith in his ability to keep the great snake down.

"Please, Jessie. Get up."

Her eyes cleared slowly. She looked directly into Ki's

94

eyes, smiled faintly, and then, as consciousness returned with a rush, fear leaped into her eyes.

"Jesus!" she whispered.

"Exactly. Please unwind it from your body, Jessie."

She did so, hating the touch of the thing. It was heavy, very heavy; that still surprised her. She lifted the tail and then scooted it under her, around again and over while Ki watched, small beads of perspiration on his forehead, his grip ferocious as he pinned the snake's head.

"Who would do something like this?" Jessie made a deeply disgusted sound and wriggled free to stand leaning weakly against the wall, staring with revulsion at the python.

"Can you walk? Go find the snake handler, Jessie."

"Yes. He's the only one, Ki. The only one who could have brought it here. Unless..." She was going to say unless the thing had somehow escaped and made its way here purely by accident, but the coincidence was too far-fetched. "I'll go."

"Are you sure you're all right?"

"Yes. Sure." She started to pluck the derringer from behind her belt, but then she glanced at Ki. He shook his head. Neither of them wanted to kill the snake, which acted solely out of instinct. It was the person who had brought it here that Jessie wouldn't have minded plugging.

She was out the door into the fresh, cool air; the sunlight was brilliant. The big tent, she saw, was being hoisted. She found the snake handler easily, but she couldn't talk to him. Someone had caved his head in.

"Jessie!" It was John Quayle, and Jessie turned from the body.

"Help me here, please."

"What's happened?"

"I don't know. I just found him." Briefly she told him about the snake. Quayle made sympathetic and incredulous

95

noises as they examined the man on the floor.

"I don't think he's going to make it," Quayle said, but the snake handler astonished them both with his toughness. He opened an eye and said, "Yeah, who says so? Where's my damned python, anyway?"

After that he collapsed. They got him onto his bed and cleaned and bandaged, the head wound and when he came around again, they got part of a story out of him. It wasn't much. Someone had come into the wagon and hit him on the head. He didn't know who, and could provide not even a scant description. Why didn't they leave him alone, he kept muttering, he had a headache and where was his snake?

The snake was being delivered. Ki had enlisted Waldo's help, and they walked toward the snake handler's wagon, Ki holding the head, the rest of the python draped over Waldo's shoulders. It looked like some weird, primitive ceremony. No one paid much attention. In a circus they had seen it all.

They eventually got the snake back into its cage and served it a half-dozen rabbits that the trainer had caught that morning. It got to work gorging itself.

"I don't understand this," Quayle said. He stood with his arm around Jessie, supporting her. "Do you think someone was trying to kill you."

"Oh yes."

"It couldn't have been some kind of accident?" Quayle asked tentatively.

"Was the attack on the snake trainer an accident?" Ki said dryly.

"Well, maybe it was a practical joke that got out of hand. How would anyone know that the snake would attack?"

"It was half-starved—it would try to kill whatever it found itself next to," Ki said.

"It doesn't seem possible." He shook his head. "Why? Why would anyone try to kill you?"

"I don't know," Jessie said. "I always have had trouble making friends." She smiled.

Quayle didn't smile in response. He wasn't in the mood for jokes. It was difficult to tell *what* kind of mood he was in, Ki thought. One thing he did know—Quayle realized this was no joke. He realized it was an intentional attempt at murder, or at least an effort to frighten Jessie off. How Ki knew that, he could not have explained, but he knew it. He knew from looking into the blond acrobat's eyes that all was not as it seemed with John Quayle.

Quayle went on. "It would have taken two men—or one *huge* man—to carry that thing." His eyes went then to Waldo, who was standing, watching the snake swallow whole rabbits.

That was very nicely done, Ki thought—putting suspicion on Waldo. The fact was that there were other ways of getting the snake into his and Jessie's wagon than carrying it. A cart, for example.

Maybe, Ki thought further, it really was not an attempt at murder, but a try at scaring Jessie off. Maybe, he thought, looking into Quayle's blue eyes, the man really did care for Jessie too much to murder her in cold blood.

★

Chapter 10

The first show of the Oriental Knife Merchant, as Ki was now billed, was well attended. Ki had on a gold brocade robe, which he wore open, since it was too small to tie around him. Jessie had taken the white dress and cut the sleeves off. She wore it with the first few buttons open, displaying a pleasing amount of cleavage. At least the men in the Plainview audience appreciated it. They whooped and hooted. Half of them were drunk.

"Now," Ki said a little stiffly—he still wasn't used to being an Oriental Knife Merchant—"my assistant will face the Ring of Death."

He and Jessie raised their hands and Jessie spun away to take her place against the board, smiling brightly to the audience. Ki went through a little more of his spiel, briefly juggled four knives, and then began outlining Jessie with the throwing stars and the knives.

It went over well enough. The crowd applauded. What they really had hoped, Jessie thought cynically, was for one of those stars to pierce her breast. Bless the human race.

Between shows, Jessie went into town. There was still nothing from the U.S. marshal's office, and the town marshal was still in his grave, unable to help.

Ki had one idea. "If we told these people that the guns were for the Comanches, they would tear the circus apart."

"And hurt a lot of innocent performers."

"It would stop the shipment."

"This one."

Ki knew the idea wasn't much, but when the mind gets frustrated it rattles around in its cage, moving in hectic circles, grasping at straws.

It had grown warm. Lightning flickered in distant clouds. The humidity was oppressive. Ki walked to the river and took a short bath. The next show was on in an hour.

But someone had found the local talent and sent them down to take care of Ki. It was almost a duplicate of the Amarillo situation: two men, half drunk, wearing low-slung, ill-cared-for Colts. They stood on the bank of the creek, watching him.

"Got a message for you, Chink," said the big one, the one with the salt-and-pepper whiskers, premature gray hair, and a twisted nose.

"Yes?" Ki answered. "What is it, please?"

"Come on out. You got to come out to hear it." The two of them snickered together, and Ki rolled his eyes skyward. How many oafs like these were there in this state?

"If you have a message, please tell me now. If not, please go away," Ki said.

"Sure." The smaller one, who had a folded ear and a shock of red hair, stepped to Ki's clothes and kicked them into the creek. Both men had a good laugh out of that. "Get the message, China boy?"

"Yes," Ki answered almost with regret. "I get the message." Lightning crackled again. The skies were teeming with colorless clouds. It would rain or worse—the weather was very unstable...

"He's not listening, Harry," the smaller man said.

"No. He's not too smart, are you, China boy?"

"How much are you being paid?" asked Ki, still waist-deep in the water.

The question threw the bullies into momentary confusion. Finally the big one asked, "Why?"

"Because it isn't enough. Not enough to die for. Perhaps you are in need. Have you no jobs? I can give you a little to tide you over."

"The sonofabitchin' China boy is trying to buy us off!" Harry laughed. "No, sir, Chink. We was paid to do the job, and by God we give satisfaction."

There was no point in delaying things. The men wouldn't go away, and soon they would perhaps get the idea of potshooting at Ki while he bathed. That would no doubt appeal to their tiny minds.

Besides, he had a second show in an hour.

Ki walked toward the bank naked, and the bullies engaged in some more nudging and snickering. He was tired beyond endurance of this sort of mentality. They inhabited saloons and back alleys, feeling alive only when they were injuring something else. Ambitionless, aimless, they were scarcely human, despite their ability to speak in a rudimentary way.

"What do you want?" Ki asked.

Again the thugs burst into laughter. "You are leaving, boy. You are leaving now. On your feet or laid out, but you are leaving Plainview."

"That is the message?"

"That's it, China boy."

"May I ask who sends the message?"

"That don't matter. We're the ones that are telling you. So it's your decision."

"My decision?" Ki was watching their gun hands.

"That's right. You leave upright or reclining. Which is it?" the big man asked.

"I choose to stay in Plainview," Ki said. "Now go on away and tell whoever sent you that you have failed."

"Damn," the smaller man chuckled, "he's got heart, ain't he? A shame to do this."

He drew his pistol, but the movement was awkward and slow. Ki had been watching for it. He sprang, rising in a leaping kick that snapped the gunman's wrist and sent the gun flying. Ki landed, went to a crouch, and came up, wrists crossed, eyes alert.

Harry already had his gun out. Instinct had caused him to step back three paces, out of Ki's range. The bore of the big Colt in Harry's hand looked like a tunnel mouth. Harry's eyes were narrow and hard. Ki thought he could roll forward and come up . . . but the odds were bad and the thought was broken off by the appearance of an ally.

From out of the trees the warrior came, a blur in dark silk, hands and feet flashing too quickly for the untrained eyes to follow. But Ki saw it, saw the knee to the groin and the following blow, a straight, intensely focused thrust of a fist to the bully's belly, which lifted Harry from his feet, eyes protruding, mouth pinched together in silent pain.

He hit the ground and lay there, his twitching feet stirring up tiny puffs of dust, his contorted face pale and strained as he gasped for breath. Ki's man had gotten up and run into the trees, holding his shattered wrist.

Ki turned how to face Chan Li.

"Te," he said. "You know open-handed fighting."

101

"I know a little. My father was a warrior." She shrugged, looking Ki up and down. "Dress yourself, Ki. What a shame you are."

"Yes," Ki said, picking up his clothes, slipping them on as he studied the small woman before him.

"You surprised me, that's all. I had no idea you were so dangerous. You certainly didn't seem so when I first met you, though you were angry enough."

She smiled grimly. "Surely you, of all people, know how important it is not to let one's skills become too visible too soon. And I must admit, I really did not want to scare you away, bad Japanese demon that you are." She stepped forward, helped Ki button up his shirt, and kissed his chest at the base of his throat. "I'm only dangerous to my enemies, and you are not my enemy."

And you, Ki thought, *are not mine—I hope.*

The second show was a repetition of the first. Jessie thought Ki was beginning to enjoy himself, plucking knives out of his sleeves, flourishing them grandly.

There was again no wire for her when she went into town before the last performance.

It had begun to rain with nightfall, and the turnout was smaller for the evening show. Jessie and Ki went through their act and then began packing up, changing into their traveling clothes. Only a few of the *shuriken* were put away in their trays in the wagon. The others were placed in the various pockets of Ki's leather vest. The time was approaching when *te* would not be enough, when the "open hand" would have to be filled.

The rain was savage but brief, gouting down out of a lightning-rent sky, accompanied by thunder like cannonades. It stopped as quickly as it had begun, and by morning the water had nearly been soaked up by the thirsty plains.

At dawn the circus train rolled out, westward and south-ward toward the secret empire a handful of madmen were building.

There was water running in the arroyos, so there was no need to worry about the animals for the time being. The land ahead was raw and dull brown, with only here and there a slash of green where grass grew in a protected canyon or willows clustered along the seasonal streambeds.

Ki was silent as he drove. He had informed Jessie about the events of the day before, about Chan Li coming to his aid. He hadn't wanted to tell her, but it might be necessary for Jessie's own safety that she know. And as much as Ki had come to like Chan Li, nothing in the universe could distract him from his first duty, his duty to Jessica Starbuck.

"It means nothing," Jessie had told him.

"No."

"No more than the odd way John Quayle acts at times."

"You are quite right, Jessie."

Then they shared a silent thought, a concern that they had both become quite foolish simply because they did not *want* people whom they liked to be hardened killers.

Jessie had had enough of the wagon bench. After noon-ing, she borrowed a horse from the Taylor twins, who were young, redheaded, and affable, and went riding.

"Jessie, with each mile we move toward Comanche coun-try," Ki warned her.

"I'll be careful," she promised. "I'm not going out far, anyway."

Jessie waved a hand and then heeled her horse forward. A longlegged, deepchested blue roan, the gelding was eager to run. It stretched out its neck and ran across the grassy plains, leaving the circus caravan behind. Jessie's hair blew out behind her. The wind was fresh and cool in her face. She cantered for half an hour, letting the horse have its head.

When she slowed the horse to a walk, they were nearly out of sight of the circus train.

No farther, then. No sense worrying Ki.

She led the horse for a way, stretching her legs. The wind was at her back. The long grass was flattened by it. A narrow silver rill traced its way southward.

She came upon it quite unexpectedly—a hollow deep enough to hide a mounted man, a sort of crater perhaps twenty feet deep, carved into the plains. It was all of a hundred feet long, ovoid, carpeted with new green grass.

It was simple enough to see how the hollow had been formed. In former times it had been a buffalo wallow, and the creek running into it and out again had elongated and deepened it.

That much was obvious, easily understandable.

More difficult to understand was why a dozen men had been concealed there.

Jessie frowned, rested a hand reassuringly, briefly, on her belt gun, and went on down into the hollow; the roan moved lazily after her, head bobbing.

Down in the hollow she confirmed what the tracks above had told her. There had been a dozen of them, all white, not Comanches—their horses were shod, and they men had smoked many cigarettes as they waited for something or somebody.

She could see spade-shaped footprints. They had worn high-heeled boots. Here and there the buttplate of a rifle had left its distinctive mark in the rain-softened soil.

Jessie wasn't an Indian scout, a practiced tracker, but she had eyes good enough to see what was happening here.

What for? she asked herself. *Following the circus?* Beyond doubt, following the circus. Two immediate explanations occurred to her.

The first was that members of the Cheney-Cruz army had been watching the weapons the wagons carried, making sure they arrived at their destination.

The second was that men had been hired to remove the two people who were trying to stop the shipment. There were a lot of them for that, but sending them out two at a time hadn't been working too well. Ki was capable of handling them by pairs until doomsday.

Jessie didn't like the feel of things. The wind was cool, but there was a deeper chill creeping up her spine. She swung aboard the blue roan and started it southward, riding up and out of the hollow and onto the flats.

Southward she rode, seeing the dots of color which were the wagons.

And she was riding in someone's tracks.

She couldn't have missed them, lined out arrow-straight from the hollow toward the trail the circus was following— the tracks of a single horseman obvious in the long grass. Jessie lifted her eyes toward the distance, but saw no one. The meeting had taken place an hour or so ago, apparently.

She rode more slowly now, looking for a patch of rain-softened bare ground where a good imprint might have been made. Her patience was rewarded. Dipping down across a narrow gulley, she found a place where the horse, slowed to a walk to cross, had left clear imprints of all four hooves.

"I won't miss that one," she muttered, crouching down to study the tracks. The right forefoot had a built-up shoe. It toed slightly in, as well. Very distinctive and very uncommon. The horse would be easy to find; the rider, if he was clever, would be a little more difficult.

The rain began again. It was like someone drawing a drape across the sky. The world went dark and the skies opened up, rain hammering down as lightning smeared gaudy light against the silver and black clouds. Jessie let the roan stretch out its neck once more. She made a run for the circus as the wind blustered and thunder rumbled.

The wagons continued to roll. Jessie rode up beside their own wagon, and stepped nimbly from the stirrups and onto the wagon seat, holding the reins of her mount like a lead rope.

She told Ki briefly what she had seen.

"That is not good. The odds against us are increasing," he said worriedly.

"They couldn't get much worse," Jessie said.

"No." Ki smiled thinly. Lightning slashed the skies again. The wind drifted his dark hair across his eyes. "You found no indication who it was that rode out there?"

"No. There was a confusion of tracks where he—she?— dismounted."

"But you'll know the horse?"

"I'll know the horse."

Ki nodded. The rain was nearly blinding now. The ground beneath the wagons was suddenly very soft, and somewhere up ahead someone had bogged down. The line of wagons stopped, and Jessie and Ki sat staring through the rain at the colorful, pathetic, deadly little caravan.

Howell came by on his white horse ten minutes later. "Broke an axle on the Wallers' wagon. We're going to camp here." Before Ki could ask him a question, Howell was gone, repeating the same message to the next wagon in line.

Jessie climbed down and went to the back of the wagon to find her rain slicker and Ki's; this time the storm didn't seem likely to let up for a while.

It was around four o'clock, but it was nearly dark. The wagons were roughly circled and the horses had been un-hitched and the cooking fires started with some difficulty.

Jessie returned the roan to the Taylor sisters and refused an invitation to dinner. She had other things on her mind. Such as a horse with a built-up shoe on its right forefoot.

The rain covered her as she moved slowly around the camp, from wagon to wagon, pausing to casually inspect the horses she encountered. It was simpler than it sounds. The saddle horses weren't numerous. Those that had been in harness all day obviously had no interest for Jessie.

The rain washed off her hat, forming a silver, beaded curtain as it ran from the brim. It pounded at her shoulders, closed out the light of day, and screened the reddish, shifting fires beyond.

She found the horse without much trouble. It didn't make her very happy.

It was tied to the tailgate of the Quayles' wagon.

That left Jessie with three possible conclusions to choose from. The first was that John Quayle had ridden out that afternoon to talk to a band of men who were following the circus. The second was that Dorothy Quayle had done it. The third that someone had taken their horse.

She didn't like it, but it was difficult not to lean strongly toward the first supposition.

She saw them before they saw her, and Jessie pressed herself back against the wagon, easing around the corner, her eyes alert and alive.

A man and a woman, and only John Quayle moved liked that. It was Dorothy who was talking.

". . . you get rid of her or I will."

"Be sensible. How can I do it out here?"

"She's fouling up the whole operation. Her and that Chinaman of hers."

"There's nothing to be done about it, Dorothy. Just forget it." The next words struck home. "Why I ever married you, I don't know."

Dorothy shot back some flip answer that Jessie didn't hear. They went inside the wagon and closed the door, leaving Jessie in the rain.

"Damned fool," she chastised herself. She knew now, didn't she? She had wanted to know, and now she did. John Quayle was the one. And Dorothy Quayle was his wife. Both of them were in on it.

She moved swiftly off through the falling rain, toward her own wagon. If she had looked back, however, she would have seen Waldo the strongman stop and stare at the Quayles' wagon.

Chapter 11

The storm ranted on all night. It was still raining and thundering when Jessie rolled out of bed, hardly rested after a night's tossing and turning. Ki peered out gloomily.

"Very bad weather. Will we travel?"

"He wants to get there pretty bad. And if there's flooding ahead of us, we won't get there at all."

"You're right. Howell will want to travel. Even if it is impossible."

It wasn't exactly impossible, but it was as close as one could get. Rain drove down like steel rods out of a black and rolling sky. Iron-gray puddles of water spotted the plains. The wind whipped Jessie's dark rain slicker as she hitched the horses and stood staring into the teeth of the storm, trying to quiet the nearside horse, which almost jumped out of its skin each time lightning flashed, and that was happening with increasing frequency.

Ki found Howell having a conference with the other performers. "We are going to travel on, people," the circus manager said loudly.

One of the Taylor twins said, "This is ridiculous."

"There's bound to be water running in the gulleys," said Verdugo, who trained the big cats.

Ben, the elephant handler, was adamant. "I can't move my animals in this weather."

Ki saw John Quayle standing and listening, his hat tugged low and tied down, water glossing his yellow rain slicker. Behind him stood Waldo in a raincoat that was bursting at the shoulder seams.

"Listen, people, we're going to get wet whether we stay here or move on. I don't see any point in waiting. Maybe the streams ahead are swollen. Maybe they're not yet. We've got to keep moving."

"I want my time, then," the Taylor girl said. "I'll go back to Plainview and sit out the winter."

There wasn't much steel in her threat. Go back to Plainview and do what? Get a job in a dance hall? There was a lot more grumbling, but Howell's decision was made, and in the end everyone gave in. If this storm kept up much longer they wouldn't be giving in, they'd be in a lynching mood.

Verdugo went off muttering about food for his cats. He had several oxen with him for that purpose, but he had counted on shooting some game on the way to supplement that. Ki waited as they drifted away one by one. Finally he was left alone with the blond man.

"Death Angel," Ki said, moving in.

"What?" John Quayle smiled. "How are you, Ki? Jessie all right?"

"We have something to settle."

"We do?" Quayle seemed genuinely puzzled, and Ki frowned. Was he or wasn't he?

"We know who you are."

"You do?" Quayle shrugged slowly. "Well, that's that, then."

110

"So it must be you and me. To the death."

Quayle just stood looking at Ki, obviously not understanding. "Not to the death. Not at all. Which side are you on, Ki? Maybe I've got you wrong. I always thought the Starbucks stood for something in this part of the country."

"The Starbucks have, always. And you, what do you stand for?"

"You said you knew."

"I am in no mood for playing games."

"I can't talk about it out here." The wagons were starting to roll. People were moving hurriedly toward their positions. "Tonight at my wagon," Quayle continued. "Bring Jessie along. We'll have this out."

"She knows Dorothy is your wife."

Quayle was momentarily struck dumb. "She's a good little detective, isn't she?"

"She is good," Ki said slowly. "Simply good."

"All right. We've got to talk. Tonight." Quayle's wagon was starting to roll, his wife at the reins. He lifted a hand and dashed off through the storm. Ki stood staring. Then he shook his head and walked thoughtfully toward his own wagon.

"Where were you?" Jessie asked, handing him the reins as he climbed up.

"Talking to Quayle."

"Did you . . . was there a fight?"

"Nothing. I don't think he is the man, Jessie. I don't understand it, but I don't believe he is the Death Angel."

"The evidence . . ."

"We misunderstand. It must be so." The brake was recalcitrant, swollen perhaps by the dampness. Ki stood up and leaned on the handle to free it. When he went to sit down again he saw the *shuriken* imbedded in the wooden wagon bench, precisely where he had been seated.

"Ki!" Jessie cried in amazement. She had her derringer

111

out; her eyes searched the storm, but there was no one visible. The wagon directly in front of theirs was that of the Taylor twins, and it hadn't even a back door or window.

"Did you see where it came from?"

"I didn't see anything."

"Move it!" Howell, on his white horse, was beside their wagon, gesturing wildly with his arm. "Let's get it rolling here, knife-thrower."

"Yes," Ki said, his eyes narrowing as he studied Howell. He was the one nearest, the one with opportunity, but it didn't seem that Howell could be the killer they wanted. But then maybe he was that good at camouflage.

The team started forward through the rain. Jessie started to remove the *shuriken,* but Ki placed his hand on hers. "No, Jessie. Knowing this man . . . do not touch it with your bare hand."

She looked closer and saw the tarlike resin on the points of the throwing star, and she knew Ki was right. The *shuriken* had been treated with poison. Ki pried it free with his belt knife, examined it briefly, and then threw it away into the mud.

"Ki—"

"I don't know."

"You must have an idea who it is."

"I have no idea. Maybe after we talk to Quayle we will know more."

"We're going?"

"Of course. But we shall go cautiously," Ki said with a tight smile. He tugged his hat down and hunched forward, watching the rumps of the team as they slogged though the downpour.

The rain lightened up a little at noon, but it was too late for that to help much. The creek they had stopped at was swollen with raging white water. Howell stalked up and down, cursing and growing red in the face.

112

"How deep is that, anyway?"

"Not so very deep," Schupe said, "but with the water moving like that—"

"Three feet, four feet?"

Verdugo tried to explain. "That water's got the force of a locomotive behind it, boss. We can't cross it. If you've never tried it, you wouldn't guess how much power's there."

"Take the lead wagon over," Howell bellowed.

"We can't—"

"And what are we going to do? Go back? Then what happens? There's a big payday ahead of us, dammit!" Howell shouted.

The first wagon was the Taylor sisters'. One of the twins stood up in the box, hands on hips, and shrilled back at Howell, "If you think I'm taking my wagon into that creek, you're crazy! I wanted to go back to Plainview, and I was right."

"Shut up. Knife-thrower, you take yours across."

Ki looked at the rolling white river and shook his head. "It will not work, Mr. Howell. I do have a suggestion, though, if Ben thinks the elephants will cross that stream."

"My animals?" Ben objected.

"They could pull the wagons through," Ki said.

"Maybe. Maybe so." Ben was meditative. "They can walk that creek, all right. If they feel like it."

"Dammit, let's have a try at it," Howell said. "Before it's too late."

Howell was getting panicky, and with good reason. The water was still rising. You could almost see the river spreading out, engulfing more and more land.

Ben was up on his bull elephant, walking it toward the river. The elephant balked, but Ben yanked at its ear and it went on into the swollen stream, the other elephants following, trailing towlines.

In fifteen minutes the first wagon was ready to cross.

113

The Taylor twins' rig was stabilized with lines on either side. It went forward slowly into the current and was buffeted roughly, the horses momentarily losing their footing before Ben, on the far side, walked his lumbering charges forward and the wagon was drawn smoothly across.

In an hour and a half they were all across. No one had much heart to go on, but Howell was adamant. "How many more streams are we going to have to cross?" Verdugo grumbled. "We're cut off now, you know? Cut off good and proper. We have to go forward. That's what he wanted all along. He was afraid of us voting to turn back."

Verdugo may have been right. Everyone but Howell was in a lousy mood. They rolled on, the wheels of the wagons sinking deep into the mud of the plains.

Night camp was made on a patch of barren ground without shelter or definition in the darkness. The big cats were restless. Their roars competed with the rattling thunder. Two windblown fires had been built, and over these they cooked supper.

Jessie and Ki ate lightly, and when it was time, they went to the Quayle wagon. The door opened and Dorothy Quayle's head appeared. "Come on," she said with disgust, stepping back. Jessie went in first, and Ki followed. Quayle was sitting on his bed, smiling up at Jessie.

"Cards on the table, is that it?"

"That's it," Jessie said, "and time enough, don't you think?"

"It's time, I suppose. We're working at cross purposes here."

Dorothy Quayle was leaning against the far wall, her arms folded, her eyes penetrating. Jessie and Ki were offered seats, but both declined.

"Who are you?" Ki asked, and John Quayle showed him the star.

114

"A Texas Ranger?"

"Afraid so," John said. Dorothy was still glowering.

"You had better, perhaps, explain this to us," Ki suggested.

"Yeah, I think so. Roughly, this is what happened. Someone came to the Rangers with a story about somebody trying to take over a part of Texas and New Mexico with force of arms. A foreign power."

"Hardly a job for the Rangers."

"Maybe, but no one else was doing anything about it. On the surface, the story was absurd. A circus carrying an army of revolutionaries? No sense to it at all. Captain Jennings thought we should have a look, a short look anyway. He called me up from San Angelo."

"Why you?"

"It's obvious, isn't it? As a child I was with a circus. When my parents died I worked on for a while, got tired of it, took up a badge and a gun. I could get into shape, pass with a circus, a second-rate one—my days as a great aerialist are gone, if they were ever here."

"You and Dorothy," Jessie said leadingly. Dorothy smiled very sweetly at her; that smile could have killed. "Your wife?"

"Not anymore," Quayle said. "We were married in the old days, the circus days. It was annulled after only ten days."

"Yet Dorothy came?" Ki said.

"Well, I needed a partner. Who was I going to get? She knew my act. She was good enough to do it."

"Second biggest mistake of my life," Dorothy Quayle said. "Damned fleabitten circus, a thousand miles of empty land."

No one asked her why she had done it. Jessie thought it was obvious; she had wanted John Quayle back. He might

115

have thought it was long over, but Jessie would have bet that Dorothy didn't feel that way. It explained the poisonous looks.

"We're nearly out of Texas," Ki said, "if not already. How long can you stay with the circus?"

Quayle shrugged. "I'm committed now. I don't see the sense in pulling out. I was ready to pull off back in Amarillo. I wasn't making any progress, and as you say, it was pretty obvious Howell was leaving Texas. Then I found some hard evidence. Rifles. I guess you know about them."

"Yes."

"So I wired the captain I was sticking with it."

"But not alone," Jessie said, lifting her eyes, and Quayle smiled a little sheepishly.

"No, not alone. How'd you find out?"

"I was out riding and I saw your tracks."

"I have twelve men with me, following the circus. If things get tough, they'll come in."

"Do you know how many men you are facing?" Jessie asked.

"No."

"Sit down a minute, John. Let me fill you in on what we've found out."

And she did, telling Quayle about Cruz and Cheney. He knew both names very well, but he hadn't known about the cartel or about the Death Angel, and he grew silent and pale as Jessie told him.

"I had thought this was just some kind of border gang," Quayle told them. "I figured if twelve Rangers couldn't handle it, an army couldn't. Damn," he breathed.

"There are more of us than before," Ki pointed out. "We do not have an army, but we can fight. We must stop this before it has time to take hold."

"That's easy for you all to say," Dorothy said, her voice

116

grating and sharp. "I just took up this job to help John on some lousy investigation. I didn't sign up to go to war."

John muttered soothing words while Jessie and Ki exchanged a glance. Dorothy Quayle had perhaps heard too much, considering her apparent instability.

There wasn't any point in worrying about that. Dorothy would want to turn back—who wouldn't? Half the people in the circus train wanted to turn back, but events had conspired to make that just about impossible. It was raining like hell outside again, and the streams were running full. Tough for Dorothy, tough for everyone.

"We can't expect any help, then?" Quayle asked.

"No. I was trying to get through to the U.S. marshal, but I never got a response."

"Funny, unless the wires were being intercepted." And that too was possible. The cartel had people everywhere. "And there's not even any point in making plans about what we're going to do when we get there, is there?"

"We can only do as circumstances dictate," Ki answered.

"If we could find this Death Angel and put him out of the way, it would help. Oh"—his head came up—"you must have thought that was me."

"Only briefly," Jessie said. "We haven't been able to discover who he is."

"*What* is he?" Dorothy asked. "Some kind of gunfighter?"

"Much more dangerous, I am afraid," Ki said. "A man skilled with all weapons, and not just handguns. Skilled with weapons and without weapons. A barehanded killer, if need be." Dorothy shuddered a little, displaying a good imagination. Ki approved. Let her take it all very seriously.

"If this weather keeps up," Quayle put in, "we may not have a case at all. We'll be very lucky to reach our destination—you don't have that pinpointed?"

117

"No."

"I thought not. Well"—he shrugged—"that's that. Any point we haven't covered?"

Nobody could think of one. It was getting late, and Ki hadn't eaten. He turned to Dorothy Quayle. "Would you like to eat? They have pitched a small tent. It's quite dry inside."

Dorothy looked at Jessie and then at her ex-husband. "What the hell," she growled, "I might as well."

Ki opened the door, letting in the cold, gusting rain, and Dorothy, putting on her rain slicker, went on out ahead of him.

"Well?" John Quayle said as the door closed.

"Well what?"

Jessie stepped to him, her body slumping against his as John's hands reached down and gripped her hips, pressing her to him. "Aren't you going to apologize?" he asked.

"For what?"

"For making a killer out of me."

"I never really . . ." She laughed and shrugged and went to tiptoes to kiss him. "Well, I apologize."

"You'll have to pay for that, you know," he teased.

"Oh yes? How?"

He was preparing to show her when thunder crashed near at hand and a shrill scream of pain sounded from outside. And then they both realized it wasn't thunder at all, but the rolling peal of gunfire.

Chapter 12

Quayle leaped for one of the heavy wooden trunks and threw it open. Jessie had her own belt gun with her, but she was only too grateful to accept the Winchester that Quayle pulled from beneath the folded clothing and handed to her. She checked its load as Quayle pulled out a second rifle for himself. Then they nodded to each other and headed for the door.

They hadn't quite reached it when it burst open and a rain-drenched, weirdly painted apparition leaped inside and fired a wild shot from the rifle he carried. The explosion was deafening in the enclosed space, and the bullet shattered a wall mirror.

Quayle didn't give the Comanche time to lever another round. He fired once, and his shot wasn't wild.

The Indian caught the slug in the face, and its impact snapped his head back and blew him backwards out through the door, where he landed with a splat in the mud. Outside, fire danced against the night skies. Rain fell into the writhing flames, but the fire refused to be extinguished.

Quayle glanced at Jessie. "Stay in here," he said.

"Like hell. I've been through a fight or two. I can't help if I'm in here."

John started to argue. It didn't do any good. Jessie was past him and out into the rainy night.

The gunfire was continuous. Some two dozen mounted Comanche warriors rode through the camp, whooping, firing in all directions. They took some answering fire and then were gone, to circle back and storm through the camp again. Jessie saw someone down in the mud. She thought it was Bertolli, the India Rubber Man, but she wasn't sure.

She saw Ki near the tent that had been pitched to shelter the cookstove, and screamed out a warning as she saw a yellow-daubed Comanche launch himself from horseback at her companion.

But Ki knew the Indian was there—felt it, perhaps— and he turned, crouching, coming up with a sideways kick that caught the Comanche in the chest and stopped him dead, bursting his heart.

"Jessie!"

At Quayle's shout, Jessie turned. She had been watching Ki, and not her own position. A Comanche on a pinto pony was nearly on top of her. His eyes were lighted by fire and lust. He had raised his war lance to strike, then seen a prize as Jessie turned—a prize he did not want to kill, but to take to his lodge.

He had made a mistake. Jessie lifted the Winchester and put a bullet through his chest. He tumbled from the back of his war horse.

Jessie spent too much time watching that warrior; two more were behind her, on foot, silent and eager. She heard the harsh, close breathing, the groping hands, and she turned,

120

trying to club them off. When the rifle was torn from her hands, she tried to go for the eyes, her fingers clawing. The Comanche ducked away from the attempt and Jessie tried a knuckle punch at the second Comanche's larynx. She caught him only a glancing blow as she was turned and hurled to the ground, her blouse front tearing free in the grasp of the Comanche. She looked toward Ki, but he was not there. John had circled the wagon, leaving her alone.

Alone but for the hulking shape that appeared out of the darkness. It picked up the Comanche to Jessie's left and shook him as a cat might shake a mouse, then hurled him headfirst into the side of a wagon. The Indian bounced off, lifeless, and crumpled into the mud.

Then the shape reached out with one huge hand and took the Comanche that was hovering above Jessie by the throat. The Indian's eyes bulged and his mouth opened, the tongue protruding grotesquely. Then the shape reached out with its other hand, grasped the Comanche's head, and twisted. Jessie winced and turned away at the snapping and cracking of cartilage and bone as the Indian's neck was broken and he folded, looking almost boneless, to the ground.

Waldo stood there huge and dark in the rain, shuddering, his shoulders rising and falling with primitive emotion. Jessie was up on her feet now, and Waldo placed his raincoat around her shoulders.

"Thank you."

He didn't answer, but just walked away, muttering in a language that seemed only semihuman. Jessie had her Winchester again. The attack seemed to have broken off. There was only sporadic firing from the west side of the camp. Probably nothing was being hit. The circus people—with exceptions like Colonel Payne, the sharpshooting expert—were not and could not be expected to be good shots.

John was there suddenly, out of the darkness. He looked at Jessie, saw the mud on her, the huge raincoat, and he knew.

"Are you all right?"

"Yes."

"Damn me, I shouldn't have left you."

"It's all right, John. I'm all right."

"Was it Waldo?" Quayle asked.

"Yes," she answered with some surprise. "He helped me."

"I thought so." They walked through the mud and rain toward the cooking tent. Ki was there, watching. A wounded man was being taken inside the tent. Lightning crackled again across a dark and roiling sky.

They were nearly to Ki before Quayle said, "You know it's him, don't you? You know that Waldo is the Death Angel."

"Yes," Jessie said. "I guess I've known it for some time."

"You both seem sure," Ki said. "But I'm not."

Jessie told him how Waldo had handled the two Indians, and Ki responded, "It was not *te,* not *jujutsu.*"

"Maybe not. You call it what you like. He knows how to kill," Quayle said.

"We can't stand around discussing it now," Jessie reminded them. "Let's see what the damage is, and who's in charge."

"The Comanches won't be back. Not tonight."

"Perhaps not," Jessie answered. "But would you stake your life on it?"

Quayle shrugged and grinned, and they started off through the camp. It was a little grim just now. Two people were dead, and the tightwire walker, a man named Ernst, looked as if he wasn't going to make it. There was an arrow through his body, penetrating the liver, from the looks of it.

Howell was in a daze, walking around with his pistol dangling in his hand, mud smeared over his trousers and shirtfront. He looked up as Jessie, Ki, and Quayle approached.

"Why, I never thought they'd come at night," he said. The rain washed down over him. His pomaded dark hair was in a matted tangle. "This is serious. Very serious."

It was more than that, but Howell was in shock just then, and having trouble with his words.

"Where is everyone?"

"In the cooktent."

"That's no good. You saw how they fired the wagons. The tent will go like nothing."

"In this rain..."

"Anyway, it doesn't provide a hell of a lot of shelter from bullets. We stay inside and they just shoot through the tent. If they've got enough ammunition, we're all dead."

"I didn't think they'd come at night," Howell said again. "I can't turn back, don't you see!" He gripped Quayle's shirtfront and looked at him pleadingly.

"Why not?"

"Because I—"

"You already took their money?"

"Yes." Howell didn't even seem surprised by the question. Perhaps he was too scared to be surprised. "You don't know how they are! If I don't go through with this, they'll kill me! They'll destroy the circus and everyone with it. I know they will." He repeated, "I can't turn back."

It's not very important right now," Ki said. "what you feel you must do. It is physically impossible to return, I believe. The creeks are much too high. And there is no reason to believe there is more security from the Comanches in that direction than in this one."

"I was in debt," Howell said, still trying to justify him-

123

self. "It's hard to make a profit in this business. The top acts cost money. I was down twenty thousand and working through my second bank loan..."

But no one was listening. "We've got to tighten up the wagon circle," Quayle said. "Put everyone inside and sit it out for tonight."

"Any chance of your men helping?" Ki asked.

"They should have been here by now," Quayle said uneasily.

"Perhaps they couldn't hear above the storm."

"Maybe not. We knew that if a situation like this came up, we were compromised, but they were told to come in if we were hit by Comanches."

Ki asked the last question of Howell. "How long has Waldo been with you?"

"Waldo?" Howell shook his head in confusion. "Not long. Maybe a week before John got here. Last month."

Ki and Quayle glanced at each other. It seemed the trapeze artist was right. It had to be Waldo, didn't it? Then why had he been protecting Jessie instead of doing the job himself? Protecting her from whom? Damn it, something was still wrong.

"Get the wagons turned. No, don't bother with the horses. We'll shoulder them around. If there are any spare weapons, get them handed around." Which was funny, considering that the circus wagons were loaded down with rifles. But to get at them, they still had to get past the big cats. No problem for Cheney. Simply shoot the tiger, the caged lion, and the big panther, and walk in and unload.

Colonel Payne, the sharpshooter, had a stock of weapons, although he didn't much like handing them out—fancy weapons with silver engraving and carved stocks. The roustabouts were the first armed. Good, solid working men, they were Texans for the most part, men with muscle in their shoulders, who had done some fighting in their time.

"I can shoot," Dorothy Quayle said, and the self-styled colonel grudgingly handed her a fine British-made target rifle and a box of cartridges.

The wagons were pushed together to form a circular barricade. Waldo was there working, his massive strength moving one wagon nearly unaided. There was no expression at all on his dull face. Tiny and expressionless eyes still stared out from under his beetling shelf of brow.

The rain began in earnest again, and they settled in for the long, long night.

The Comanches came again two hours later. Still hoping for easy pickings, apparently, they swarmed out of the night and rain toward the circus wagons. They had elected to abandon their horses.

Jessie sighted on a man wearing a buffalo robe, watching him wave his war hatchet, hearing him scream above the bluster of the cold storm.

There was a shot to her left, and Jessie triggered a round almost simultaneously. She saw her man do a half-somersault and lie still in the mud. Then she switched her sights to a Comanche on her right, fired, missed, swallowed a soft curse, and fired again.

This time it was no miss. The warrior went down in a heap, his death scream shrill and terrible. Then that too was washed out by the wave of gunfire all around Jessie. Many guns, the smoke strong and acrid even in the rainy night, the roar of doom, fire lashing out at the attackers. And then dead silence.

Nothing moved. She remained where she was, kneeling behind the wagon tongue, watching the dark, treacherous night. There was no one there. Even the dead had gone, the two men she knew she had gotten.

She sagged back, reloaded, and sat waiting, watching until dawn.

Dawn was a wash of orange and red light across the

eastern sky, with here and there a shaft of pure golden sunlight piercing the clouds to illuminate the softly falling rain. The land was raw and empty and endless. The clouds to the north were black and still building.

Howell nearly started an insurrection when he told the gathered circus performers that they were going on to Mexico City.

"The hell I am!" one of the Taylor girls shouted. "You know how far that is?"

Howell appeared to be on the verge of telling her that they weren't actually going anywhere near that far, but Schupe, at his elbow, seemed to give him a nudge.

"This is Indian country," said Verdugo, the big cat handler. "Wild and unsettled. How the hell are we going to make it? Look at this weather! Look what happened last night!"

"There will be Indians on the backtrail. There are flooded creeks behind us." Howell was desperate. He *had* to have Verdugo. "Look—I'll guarantee your pay as if we were doing three-a-days. How's that? What are you going to make if you turn back?"

"What do we make *dead?*" the Taylor girl asked. "We're going back to Plainview. I'll sling hash before I'll let some Comanche have *my* hair to sit around and play with."

Howell moaned but returned his attention to Verdugo, promising him the moon. In the end, the Taylor sisters, the fat lady, and a dozen others, including three roustabouts who said they were going to go back to where fighting wages were paid if they were going to have to fight Comanches, all left. The others stayed, including Colonel Payne, the other roustabouts, Waldo, Chan Li—who had stood next to Ki, silent and passive throughout the debate—and Jessie's party.

"There's still time," Jessie told Dorothy Quayle.

126

The trapeze artist was standing watching the wagons roll back toward Plainview. Jessie had stepped unseen beside her. Now Dorothy's eyes narrowed and her head turned slowly toward Jessie, measuring her.

"Why would I want to go?"

"You might as well. John doesn't want you back."

"I don't give a damn if he does or doesn't!" she lied.

"Sure you do. Very much. There wasn't any other reason for you to come along, was there? You don't want to resume your career as an aerialist. Why don't you go back home?"

"Why, damn you, I'll do what I want!"

"I'm not going to give you another chance to try to kill me," Jessie said.

"To *what?*" She feigned surprise, but she wasn't very good at it. Jessie smiled.

"It was you. At least twice. How did you manage to lug that python, anyway? I'll bet your back is killing you."

"I don't know what you're talking about." She turned away, folding her arms.

"Sure you do. You love John Quayle still. All right. You're here hoping to reconcile. It didn't work. You got a little jealous. So you tried to kill me—that's not all right. I'll tell you what the choices are. You go home and I'll say nothing. One day John Quayle's coming back to Texas. You'll be there waiting; I won't. What happens then between you is your business and his."

"You're mad," Dorothy said.

"Not much. You want the second alternative?" Dorothy nodded. Belligerently, but she nodded. Jessie told her. "You stay here another five minutes and I walk over and tell John what I know—that you tried to stab me to death and would have succeeded, but for Waldo. That—let me finish—failing there, you decided to put a python in my closet. Very unique, very feminine, I thought. Would a man think of

127

that?" Dorothy tried to reply but Jessie didn't let her. "If I told John what I know, he'd either arrest you or simply despise you for the rest of his life. You'd have no chance with him after this, you know that."

"You dirty bitch!"

"I said five minutes. Don't let me detain you."

It was a good thing Dorothy didn't have a knife in her hand just then, Jessie thought. Those eyes flashed and flickered, dancing with impotent rage. Dorothy Quayle spun on her heel and walked to where John stood talking to Ki.

"I'm going back as well. Can you find me a horse?"

"But, Dorothy—"

"Please," she said through chalk-white lips.

"Sure."

They found a good horse, saddled it, and sent her after the retreating wagons.

John Quayle watched her ride, shaking his head. "She was determined to stay this morning. Changeable females!"

"That's us," Jessie agreed. Ki was giving her an odd look, so she turned away, hiding a smile.

An hour later they were rolling again, across the sodden plains, ahead of them the empire of Cheney and Cruz, the new nation the cartel was midwifing, and behind them Comanche and flood and the dead, buried in shallow graves.

Jessie rode with John Quayle, but attracted no attention; everyone was too concerned with watching the banks of clouds to be bothered about gossip.

"Where are they?" Quayle muttered.

"They're probably just cut off by the storm." She rested a hand naturally on his thigh. "They're all right."

"Maybe. I was counting on them, Jessie. What chance do we have by ourselves, you, me, and Ki?"

"I don't know. What chance did we have before? You play the odds you get. That's what my father used to say."

"When they get bad enough, there's no point in being in the game."

Quayle wasn't frightened. A man who has made his living leaping through space when a fall might break his spine, crippling him for life, who has taken up law enforcement in a savage land, doesn't scare easily. He wasn't scared, but he was wary, as he had every right to be.

They rode on for silent miles, jolting and rolling over the empty land. There had been buffalo this far south, and plenty of them, but that was long ago. Now there was only the wind, the rain, and, somewhere out there, the Comanches.

★

Chapter 13

Evening brought clearing. The clouds settled to earth and the stars filled the gaps they left in the deep velvet sky. They had rocked and rolled and sloughed along all day toward the low, serrated hills ahead of them. Howell hadn't told them a thing, but by watching his eyes it was easy to tell which way he was going, and those hills were drawing him like a magnet. They had veered away from their southwesterly course and begun following the rocky plateau toward the hills.

"This ain't the way to the border," Verdugo had complained.

"It's easier traveling," Howell had said in reply.

"The time we make here we'll lose getting back on the track," the animal trainer pointed out.

Howell had just grumbled a response, turning his white horse away from Verdugo's wagon which he shared with a large and always hungry tiger.

Schupe seemed surprised by none of this. Either he was in Howell's confidence or he was extremely phlegmatic. John Quayle was watching the backtrail as he had been doing all day. He and Jessie were mounted on saddle horses, supposedly scouting for a place to camp on the vast, barren plateau, which was rock and pond, brush and pond, rock and pond just now.

"Nothing?" she asked.

"No." Quayle was very worried. "Damn it to hell."

"It doesn't mean the Comanches got them."

"No." Quayle turned blue eyes toward Jessie. "But it doesn't look real good."

"They know they can be seen a long way off—they'll probably come up on us tonight," Jessie said, not believing a word of it. Those Texas Rangers were lost—she felt it, Quayle felt it—swallowed up by the plains.

Ahead they could see some scraggly timber, mostly cedars projecting their ragged silhouettes against the sundown sky. There was a low, reddish ridge there to cut the wind. It was as good a place to camp as they were going to find.

Howell looked that way anxiously when they reported back, as if the campsite were the end of his long quest. Most likely he was just happy to have another day under his belt, to be another day nearer to Cheney and Cruz without having his people killed.

"No Indian sign?" Schupe asked. The big bald man had stripped off his jacket. He was round and rubbery, his eyes very small. His accent continued to thicken as they drew away from civilization.

"No. We didn't see anything, though maybe that's what we should expect."

"Pardon?"

"You'll be unlikely to see them before they want you

to," Quayle said. He took Jessie's horse's reins and led it away to unsaddle. Schupe was left alone momentarily with Jessie.

"Good evening," she said, starting away.

His hand fell on her arm, something she didn't like. Jessie turned cold eyes on the circus man. "Have you found, perhaps, some more of those little silver coins, Miss Columbine?"

"No, I haven't. You're going to find my boot toe in your groin, though, if you don't let go, Schupe."

"Such a menacing female!" he said with mock terror.

"You'll find out if you don't let go."

It was a long moment before he did so. Jessie took the time to look her warning deep into his eyes before she turned away to walk through the purple dusk to her wagon. She was alone as she crossed the camp. She was alone, and she didn't know why that should seem unusual until it hit her.

"Waldo," she said under her breath. She hadn't seen the big man all afternoon. Nor, looking around, could she find him now. There was only Schupe standing, thick arms folded, watching after her.

Ki hadn't seen the strongman, either. "Not since this morning," he told her. He had brewed a cup of tea and now he sipped it in the darkness. The cooking had been done before true darkness, and now, for safety, the fires were out. "Does it mean something?" he wondered.

Quayle thought it did. "I'm afraid it means he's dead."

"Dead? But if he's the man we think he is, he wouldn't be easy to kill, and who . . . ?"

"I don't know. All I know is that it isn't hard to take a human life. What do you think, Ki? An unguarded moment, a knife in the jugular—it doesn't matter how skilled a man is in combat."

"What you say is true, but I reject the thought simply

132

because I can think of no one with a reason to kill him."

"No?" Quayle's eyebrow went up. *"We* have a reason."

"But I did not kill him. Did you?" Ki asked.

"Of course not."

"What about telling Howell," Jessie said, "riding back to look for him."

"You'd never find him in the dark. Besides," Quayle said with some bitterness, "we're well rid of him. At best he's a nuisance, at worst a coldblooded killer."

But Waldo wasn't that easy to get rid of. He would be back, and Jessie suspected that it wouldn't be long. The wagons had been drawn tightly together. Men had drawn lots and taken up shifts. But they could stare intently at the darkness of the plateau and see nothing at all. The night was blacker than black, the clouds screening out the moon and stars. After midnight it began to rain again.

After midnight Chato Cruz came.

Jessie wasn't aware of it until the door to their wagon banged open and a man with a lantern stepped in, moving to one side as the Mexican behind him entered, his rifle leveled.

Ki had sprung from his bed, naked, but he pulled up short in the face of that Winchester repeater, and the man behind it laughed.

"Madre de Dios!" Cruz said softly as he caught sight of Jessie. "Is this the one? What a woman."

She had on only a thin nightgown, one that clung to her hips and breasts, revealing plainly her lush figure. Ki was tensed, ready to strike, even if it cost him his life.

"No, Ki," Jessie cautioned.

Cruz glanced that way, his eyes dismissing Ki's threat. She knew it was Cruz even before the man introduced himself, his voice oily and mocking. Glittering eyes as black as coal, a face craggy and scarred. He wore black jeans, a blood-red shirt, and a long white scarf.

"I am Chato Cruz," he said. "Welcome to my country."

"Are we in Mexico?" Jessie asked innocently.

Cruz laughed. "No. I am afraid that is no longer my country."

Jessie had picked up a robe and was belting it on while Cruz's eyes fingered her. Beyond the outlaw she could see other lantern-bearing figures moving around like fireflies in the night. A man lay crumpled against the dark earth—one of the roustabouts.

"What is happening here?" Ki asked.

"I think you know." Cruz's eyes shifted only briefly to Ki. "Dress. We will be moving soon."

Ki returned to his mat and began dressing. Cruz moved around the wagon, searching briefly. There were few firearms, and those alone interested him and were removed. The rest of the weapons he did not understand or see as a threat, as long as he himself had a gun in his hand. He had made his first mistake.

"Nothing?" someone asked from the doorway.

"No. Only one item of vlaue," Cruz said, and again his eyes lingereed on Jessie and he smiled thinly, revealing white, even teeth. "Pardon me," he said with mock gentility, "for this unfortunate intrusion."

"Quite all right," Jessie said in carefully measured, neutral tones. She wouldn't try to soft-soap the man, but there was no point in antagonizing him unnecessarily.

"Good." Cruz laughed. "The man." He nodded toward Ki, who was taken to the door by two Mexicans. "Please check for weapons, Carlos. The man is a knife-thrower."

Carlos did just that. He found three knives and three of the six throwing stars Ki had scooped up as he dressed. He didn't find the three *shuriken* Ki had placed in the hidden vest pockets, nor did he find the *surushin* that Ki wore as

134

a belt. It simply appeared to Carlos to be a rope holding up the Oriental's pants, a common enough thing in Carlos's native land. He was happy and proud to have found the knives. Carlos, who had no front teeth and wore a mustache to cover a harelip, displayed the weapons proudly to Cruz, who waved a gesture of dismissal.

"You will be taken care of," Cruz said as Ki was led out the door. He came nearer to Jessie. His lantern-carrier smiled a dirty smile. "Hector will stay here to watch you."

Then Cruz turned, speaking rapidly in Spanish to Hector. Jessie was a Texas girl and she understood most of it. "Touch her and I'll cut your *huevos* off," was the gist.

Cruz touched his hatbrim and went out into the night, where there were sounds of crying and shouting, and deep-voiced threats. Hector lit the interior lamp and blew out his own lantern. Then he sat watching Jessie, perhaps wondering if one such use of his *hueovs* would be worth their loss.

"If you'll turn around, I'd like to dress," Jessie said.

Hector was playing *no comprendo* at the moment. Jessie repeated the request in Spanish.

"But how will I know if you have the knives too? I must watch you dress."

"You watch the wall. If Chato wants to search me, he can," Jessie bluffed. "If *you* try it, I'll tell him."

Hector frowned deeply, glanced to the door, and turned aside. It was one of Jessie's quickest dressing jobs. She managed to get the derringer in behind her belt, and to palm another half-dozen *shuriken* from the drawer.

Hector had been peeking a lot, but he didn't see her do that.

The wagon started without warning. They had been hitching the horses while Jessie dressed. Now they were rolling through the darkness toward—where? Cheney's hideout?

135

Chato's? Were they still in this together? Chato didn't act like a man who enjoyed taking orders. The wagon hit a dip, and Jessie sat down to stare at Hector as they rolled on.

She hoped: that Ki hadn't put up a fight, and that John Quayle hadn't either. If so, one or both of them would be dead. Jessie watched Hector, knowing that she could eliminate him and get away, but she didn't know what she would gain by that. She had to ride this out, to try somehow to get to the black heart of this scheme.

It was a long night. In the darkness they hit every rut and rock in their line of travel. Hector sat there bleary-eyed, watching, his mind empty except for a single carnal hope. Jessie watched the high window for hours, yet it was still somehow surprising when she noticed the gradual graying of the sky outside, the pale flush of pink that meant dawn was breaking.

She stood and went to the window, seeing the cedar trees, the deep red canyons and ridges, the long, low mesa with the dusting of green up on the caprock, the silver glint of runoff from the rain streaking its flank.

"It's not far now, is it?" Jessie said.

"No." Hector wasn't going to waste words this morning. He was sleepy and hungry.

"Behind the mesa? Or on top of it?"

"Not far."

For another few minutes Jessie watched the land pass. Red earth and broken hills, sage and chia, manzanita and ragged cedar, a scattering of bedraggled cottonwoods in the gulleys.

She returned to the bunk, sat down, and watched Hector as the miles passed. An hour later they stopped.

They had been climbing a grade, Jessie knew. For most of the past hour and a part of the one before they had been climbing. Now they had halted. They were, she guessed, on top of the mesa. From there they would have a view of the country for miles around.

It was the redoubt, the capital of the new nation, the fortress primeval, unassailable, aloof.

The sun was in Jessie's eyes when the wagon door was opened again and she was herded out to stand blinking in the glare of the day.

The mesa stood above the red desert, which ran away endlessly. To the left, the east, stood a scattering of hastily built shelters of mud-and-pole construction. The circus people were being moved gradually away from the shelters to stand together in a cluster, encircled by Chato Cruz's men. More guards were coming, some on horseback, some afoot. Jessie tried to estimate their numbers, guessed around fifty, and wondered how many others there were unseen.

"This way, please," Hector was saying. Cruz himself had disappeared. "This way, please."

"Ki!"

He was there, tall, proud, competent. He had his arms folded, his dark eyes unsmiling. He put a hand on Jessie's shoulder. "You are all right."

"Of course. It was you I worried about. I thought you might try to fight free."

"No, that would solve nothing."

"Ki?" Chan Li rushed to him breathlessly. "What is happening here? Who are these men?"

Ki just shook his head and dropped an arm around her shoulder. They could see a small coterie of armed men walking toward them. There was purpose in their eyes. The bandit named Carlos was leading them.

Ki watched them come. From the corner of his eyes he could see Quayle standing beside Jessie, his blue eyes de-

137

fiant. A little too defiant, perhaps.

"Don't lose your temper, John Quayle. It will do no good," Ki warned him.

Carlos was in front of them now, and behind him were gathered Mexican bandits of assorted sizes. One with a whiskered face and a vastly protuberant belly stood leering toothlessly at Chan Li. She met his gaze proudly and he laughed out loud.

"This one," Carlos said, pointing at Ki, "and the blond one, the pretty woman."

"The China girl?"

Carlos hesitated. He looked at Ki before deciding. "Yes, her too."

"Come on, you," the fat bandit said. He poked Ki with the muzzle of his rifle and Ki had to fall back on his own advice, reminding himself not to lose his temper when it would do no good.

Ki started walking toward the buildings across the mesa. Jessie was on one side of him, Chan Li on the other. Behind them walked John Quayle.

They were surrounded by enough guards to cut out the daylight. The wind was cool, coming with a rush over the rim of the mesa to flatten the sparse grass and briefly throttle the rain-heavy cedars that grew there in patches.

The long, low log building ahead of them was built a little better than those to the side, where Ki noticed men squatting in the morning sunlight, smoking, playing with their knives, staring in a coldly bored manner. He tried to estimate their numbers, but it wasn't possible except to figure that the barracks buildings he saw—ten of them in all—had been built to house at least two hundred men.

"Go right in," Carlos said with a sneer.

Ki had stopped at the door to the building. Outside, several horses were hitched to a clumsily made hitch rail.

Ki pulled the latch string and entered the building.

There were three rooms, apparently: The large, nearly square room in front of them, and one on either side, entered through identical right- and left-hand doors.

There was no rug on the floor, no glass in the windows opposite, through which clear blue morning light streamed, patching the wall to Ki's left with a bright rhomboid. The men were in shadow. They sat behind a long table made of rough planks.

It took a while for Ki's eyes to adjust. When they did, he saw that the man to his left, lounging in a puncheon chair, a whiskey bottle before him, was Chato Cruz. The man to the right was slight, nervous-looking. Ki figured him for Cheney.

The man in the middle was the Death Angel.

"Please come forward. This is a court of inquiry," the Death Angel said. "You will have a chance to defend yourselves before this panel. Then you will be acquitted or punished as the laws of this sovereign state dictate."

"You mean you're going to execute us."

"Why, yes," Waldo the strongman said mildly. "I should think that would be the final result."

★

Chapter 14

Jessie stood looking at the man. He was huge, purposeful, well-spoken. The dull eyes of Waldo were gone, along with the slurred speech and fumbling gestures. Before them was a well-bred, cultured, murderous giant.

"You're not really going through with this farce of a trial?" John Quayle said bitterly. "The result has already been determined, hasn't it?"

"It is not precisely a trial," Waldo answered. "More along the lines of a military tribunal, perhaps. Our country is, in a sense, a military dictatorship. And we are now in a state of war, as you will appreciate, being one of the provocateurs of this situation."

"Oh Christ," John Quayle said with disgust.

"Well you might pray," Waldo said.

Cruz was bored. "Why don't we string them up—except for the blonde? Get this over with."

"You are not approaching matters with the proper attitude, Señor Cruz," Waldo answered.

"What am I supposed to do? I am here to fight, not to play games."

"I assure you I do not play games."

Cheney was sulking. This was his war, and this was his country, damn it! He was the ruler. Ki recognized the cartel's thinking: the three elements of the revolution were represented on the panel—pacified, supposedly. The military, Cruz. The emperor, Cheney. The power behind the throne—the cartel.

"We vote, then?" Cruz asked, pouring himself a huge glass of liquor and downing it, then wiping his mouth with his sleeve. "Everybody guilty. The blonde we pardon." He grinned crookedly and leaned forward to study Jessie, who stared back coldly.

"The charges first," Waldo said.

"Ai caramba!" Cruz muttered. He slumped back on his tailbone to stare at the ceiling. Cheney fidgeted in his chair, and Jessie, watching the little man, knew that he was not quite right in the head. Waldo, however, was cool and self-assured. He was proceeding in a way that would seem quite proper to his militaristic Prussian masters. Order would be served; everyone would be slaughtered quite systematically.

"This is my court," Ray Cheney said breathily.

"Certainly," Waldo replied smoothly. "Now let us proceed. It shouldn't take long at all. The first defendant is John Quayle, a Teaxas Ranger, a spy sent to disrupt and block our revolution. He is subject to the death penalty if you agree he is a spy—as the badge in his pocket leaves little doubt."

"Why, damn you, this is the United States!" Quayle yelled.

"It *was*."

Quayle tried to leap forward, but two *bandidos* grabbed him and yanked him back.

"Vote, gentlemen?" Waldo asked without inflection.

"Death," Cruz said, sounding bored. Cheney just nodded.

"The man called Ki. A professional subversive, a hired killer—by the way, guards, if you haven't examined his clothing very closely, please do so now." He added with a smile, "The woman too, if you please."

Jessie felt her heart sink a little. The Mexicans found the *shuriken* without much trouble. Carlos held one up. "This little thing? This is a weapon?"

"Place them on the table, please," Waldo said. "Also—that belt. Remove that, will you?"

Carlos looked as confused as before, but he shrugged and removed the *surushin* and carried it to Waldo. The big man briefly examined the five-foot rope with its weighted ends.

"Yes, very clever. I once . . . well, no one wants to hear my reminiscences. Vote, please."

"Death." Cruz said from behind a yawn. Cheney nodded again. They were all very bored with passing death penalties.

"The consort Chan Li," Waldo said. "An associate of Ki's."

"I am Chan Li, only a circus magician," she said, stepping forward so that she had to be restrained. "I have done nothing. But if you kill this man, then you must kill me too."

"No!" Ki objected loudly, but Waldo had already begun replying.

"So be it. Gentlemen?"

"Death."

Waldo's eyes lifted to Jessie now, and he smiled faintly. Ki knew, then, why the strong man had protected her. He had pretended everything else, but he hadn't been pretending his admiration of Jessica Starbuck. It was incredible, but Ki realized that the massive executioner, the cartel's chief agent here, was actually in love with Jessie!

"Don't waste your time with your trumped-up charges," Jessie said. "If these people are guilty, then I'm guilty. If they're going to die, so am I."

"But it may be possible—"

"Damn what's possible. You think I'd want to live, knowing that you had killed my friends!"

"No," Waldo said with a sigh. "I suppose not."

"No need to kill the woman," Cruz said, and Waldo turned his eyes toward the Mexican. Those eyes were killing eyes, cold and hard, but Cruz either didn't notice the danger they contained, or foolishly chose to ignore it.

"Now what's holding things up?" Ray Cheney demanded, and his voice squeaked a little. "One dies, they all die."

Waldo shook his head heavily. "Yes."

"Wait a minute. I want her," Cruz said, coming to his feet.

"Sit down, Cruz."

"You don't tell me what to do, big man."

Waldo was coiled. For a moment Jessie thought he was going to rise as well. She remembered the Indian with his neck broken by Waldo's bare hands. Waldo must have had second thoughts; he must have recalled the dozen Mexican guards in the room, or perhaps his masters' instructions.

"They all die," Waldo said finally, deliberately. "The women and the Texas Ranger by firing squad. The man Ki I shall take care of myself."

"What are you talking about?" Cheney asked.

"I shall kill Ki myself."

It was sound policy, Ki thought grudgingly. Let the army see just how good their general was. But there was more to it than that. Waldo thought he was better than Ki, and he wanted to know for sure. It was a matter of pride.

"Take them to the stockade for now," Waldo said, his hand waving dismissal, and the guards turned the condemned around. If they had expected pleas, crying, weeping from those four, they were disappointed. Jessie was too angry even to speak; Chan Li was too proud to cry; the men were too busy trying to plan a future.

There has to be a way out, Ki thought, even as they were led out of the room and marched across a damp yard toward another low building beyond. There were no windows in that building, Ki noticed. Two men stood outside with rifles slung over their shoulders.

They heard a deep-throated snarl and then the crack of a gun. A roar of pain filled the day.

"They've shot the lion," John Quayle said. He had seen the shot fired, the puff of smoke as Cruz's men prepared to recover the rifles from beneath the floorboards of the cages.

Verdugo was on the ground. The animal trainer had been put there with the butt of a rifle, and now he writhed in agony. Blood painted his face, leaking through the fingers he had pressed to his forehead.

"You don't have to do that, for God's sake!" someone shouted. It was Howell, speaking with unexpected vehemence. "Tear the bottoms out of the wagons. Let us move the cats! You can't kill my tiger!"

That was all they saw of that bloody farce. The door to the stockade was opened and they were shoved into its gloomy darkness to sag against the bare earth floor.

The door was locked behind them, and they sat facing each other in the darkness.

"Well," Quayle said, "we don't have much time." And he rose to start walking around the inside of their wooden cell, checking the walls for weak spots.

"I am growing deeply disturbed," Chan Li said in her small, defiant voice. "I am afraid I shall break the arm of one of these men. Or worse."

Normally Ki would have smiled, but there was very little that seemed funny just now. The door opened again, and as Quayle turned away from the wall, the wounded man was carried in and dropped roughly on the floor.

"Verdugo!"

As they went to see to the injured man, Howell was shoved roughly inside, to stumble against the wall. After a second, the loudly protesting Schupe was brought in, and Ben, the elephant trainer, who had been roughed up as well.

"Poor Verdugo," Ben said. "Killing his cat like that." There was comradely sympathy on the elephant handler's narrow face. "How is he?"

"All right, I think. The rifle stock split his scalp. He'll have a lump and a black eye, that's all."

"This is outrageous!" Schupe was still fuming. His accent had just about completely swallowed his English by now. His complaints were loud and guttural. Finally he turned, his hands spread. "What is a man to do?"

"We have to get out, obviously," Howell said.

"Have you an idea, Mr. Howell?" Jessie asked.

"No, unfortunately."

Jessie didn't either, nor did Ki. But Howell was right—they had to get out somehow. After that, who knew? They were well guarded. The land was empty and nearly flat below them—assuming they could get off the mesa. They hadn't even seen the road up, having been locked in the wagons. Then all they would have to do was to outrace the bandits for several hundred miles, the prisoners afoot, the bandits on horseback. It didn't look good.

"How long do we have?" Jessie wondered aloud.

145

"How long before what?" Howell asked.

"Before the executions."

"Executions!"

"Yes," she said, "that was our sentence. We've been tried for treason or some such. And found guilty."

"We haven't had any trial!" Howell protested.

"Maybe they've gotten tired of the game," Jessie replied.

"And they certainly wouldn't hang us."

"No. No, they wouldn't," Jessie said a little bitterly. "They're going to use a firing squad."

"Not on us!" Howell shrieked.

She shrugged. "I don't know. I hope not." It seemed to be the only sentence that the tribunal of Cheney, Cruz, and Waldo—or whatever his real name was—knew how to hand down. They didn't have a lot of use for the circus people, now that the guns had been delivered.

"But...I did what they told me to do. I did what I promised," Howell went on, like a child who has been playing in the mud and is surprised to find himself dirty.

"How about up there?" Quayle asked from out of the blue. Ki and John were looking up toward the ceiling, which was constructed of poles, with a sort of loft above it, then a pole roof. A little light was seeping in from somewhere.

"It is possible. Can you get up there?"

Quayle grinned. "Watch me. He crouched and leaped, his strong hands finding a cross pole. He swung up and over and into the loft, standing on two parallel poles that trembled under his weight. Walking along them, he moved to where the roof slanted to the wall, where there was a small gap for air.

"Well?" Howell hissed, and Quayle glared at him.

The door opened suddenly and Carlos came in, along with Hector and six other armed men. They herded the remainder of the circus people before them. From the corner of her eye Jessie saw Quayle flatten himself against the poles, supporting himself on his elbows and toes. He was in plain view if the guards decided to look up. Jessie kept her eyes deliberately away from him.

"What is this?" Carlos was looking at her, his dark face carved into a frown. He smelled of tequila, horses, and sweat.

"What's the matter?" Hector asked.

"I don't know." Carlos shrugged. "Something," he said suspiciously.

"Something." Hector yawned. "Always something with you."

The snake handler was near Verdugo now, squatting down, looking his concern at Ben. Two of the roustabouts seemed to have been roughed up. One of them, a big red-headed Irish Texan, glowered at his captors defiantly.

"Come on," Hector ordered his men. "Work to do. Clean out the south bunkhouse. Think the new soldiers want to sleep in your mess?"

They laughed at some kind of private joke and went out, closing the door behind them. Ki went to the door, put his ear to it, and then looked to the loft, nodding.

"Say, what...?" the redheaded Texan looked to the ceiling and grinned. "We getting out of here?"

"So we hope," Ki answered.

"You know what these boys are up to?" the Texan asked. "I heard 'em talking. The sons of bitches got five hundred rifles and the men to put behind them. Outlaws and a bunch of peons from down south. They're going to take over New Mexico Territory, they think!"

It wasn't news to as many of those present as the Texan had expected. "Guess I'm slow to learn," he shrugged. "I'm Kenny Reilley. If we're fighting back, let me know. I'm ready."

147

"Joe Dawes," another roustabout said. "I'm with Kenny, and it ain't that I like to fight the way he does, but I heard some talk on the way over, too. Me, I speak a little Mex. Border grunt, you know. They're going to shoot us all, brother. Just line us up and mow us down." Someone gasped. "It looks like it's fight or die. I'd rather go with one of their throats in my grip than standing up with a blind fold over my eyes."

There was only a whisper of sound as Quayle swung down from the rafters.

He told Ki, "There's enough of a gap up there that we could slip out, one at a time. I'd have to remove a section of roof, but the way this place is built, that's no problem, believe me. They didn't waste any time on the construction."

"There's guards all around us," Reilley pointed out.

"If we could wait until nightfall, we'd have a good chance," Quayle told Ki. Jessie shook her head.

"We don't know if we *have* until nightfall."

"Look," the Ranger said, "I'd guess we have about a fifty-fifty chance of some of us getting out after dark. There's no buildings behind us up there, just some chopped-up land, a lot of rocks, a few cedars. Good cover after a hundred feet. In the daylight there isn't a chance in a million. If they let us live until dark, we've a chance to go on living. If they don't, well . . ."

There was no point in finishing the sentence. Reilley turned around with a curse. Joe Dawes was prying at the wall. Ki frowned and turned on him.

"What are you doing?"

"When they come, I want a stick in my hands."

"They will hear you."

"What do you expect me to do? Sit here and wait for them to kill me?"

148

It was a fair question. What did Ki have to offer as an alternative?

"We must try to wait it out until dark."

"There's no guarantee we'll live until dark," Dawes said.

"There's no guarantee a stick's going to keep you alive, either," Reilley pointed out. Dawes stared at him for a moment and then slowly smiled, his hand falling away from the pole he had been digging at.

"I guess not. I'm with you men. Whatever you say goes."

Verdugo was sitting up now, madder than hell. "Shot my lion. Dirty bastards. If I ever get a gun in my hands...why, I think I'd kill them all."

Jessie had drifted over near the door. On the other side of it, two guards were talking, and she could just pick up most of what they said.

"How long is this going to last?"

"Not long. Chato will kill them all soon."

"Not the copper-haired woman, I bet."

A short, dry laugh followed. "No, not the woman."

"Why don't we do it now? Why stand around in the sun?"

"Because the big *gringo* says we wait."

"That ape? When Chato gets through with him..." their voices faded away a little as they moved.

"...a big show."

"Sure. When those *indios* from down south show up, then he'll kill them. He'll want them to see what happens to anyone who betrays the revolution."

She listened for quite a while longer, but the men had fallen into a sun-induced, torpid silence. They had nothing more to say. Jessie told Ki what she'd heard.

"That makes sense," he replied. "When the new army arrives, we'll be executed in front of them. And the Death

149

Angel will have his battle with me. To impress the men."

"But we don't know when the men from the south are going to arrive," Howell complained.

"No, we don't. We can only hope it's after dark, or perhaps tomorrow."

"Damn," Howell turned away, slapping his thighs in frustration.

"You act like this wasn't all your fault," Schupe said angrily. "I told you not to deal with these people."

"You told me that until you saw cash money. Schupe, you're fired!"

No one even had the energy to laugh.

They sat and waited, waited until dark, cheering wildly, silently, for the sun in its race with the approaching army.

Chapter 15

The shadows gathered in the corners of the low stockade like gray cobwebs spun by dusk. Jessie Starbuck watched them slowly claim the light. She was still alive. They had suffered through an interminable day, waiting with each breath to hear the hand on the door latch, the order to death. But they had lived until sundown. Now there was a chance, even if it was a very slim one.

Ki was on one side of her, and on the other side, much closer, was John Quayle, who was unable to keep his eyes off the loft, off the small promise offered by that gap between roof and wall. It was a dreadful hour, with death like an untriggered guillotine hanging over her, but she had Ki and she had John Quayle. She knew that both of them were willing to give up their lives if it would save hers. Of course it wouldn't. If they died, it would do nothing to help her or the others. Still, there was a strange intimacy in that knowledge, and Jessie found strength in it.

"A few more minutes. Just a few more," said the Texan,

Kenny Reilley. There was a small answering moan from across the room; Jessie thought it issued from Howell's throat—Howell, who had been well paid to come here for his own execution.

"I can't wait," Quayle said suddenly. "I've been sitting here expecting them for six hours. Now I've got to try it."

Ki didn't try to argue with him, although his own impatience was partly under control; he had learned long ago from his master that nothing hurried was as good as something done with care. Swiftness and control were enemies. Ki wished for control always. Speed, true speed, followed practice and discipline. But Quayle, who was a hundred percent Western, could not be expected to govern himself by the same rules.

Quayle rose, and the others automatically got to their feet. The Ranger told them, "Sit down. If someone comes in, we don't want you all standing around looking up."

There was general muttering as they sat or tried to lean negligently against the walls. It was rapidly growing dark in the room. They could hardly see each other's faces. Jessie saw John Quayle walk to the side wall, leap up, and swing again into the loft.

They tried to talk of other things in soft voices. But their throats were dry as they heard Quayle pecking at the weak spot, trying to open the space between the boards.

"Do you want help?" Ki asked from directly underneath Quayle, his voice conversational, not carrying.

"Not yet."

"How long?" Howell asked.

Ki led him away by the elbow. "Sit down, Howell. Please."

"But I want to know—"

"Yes. We are all uneasy, but please try to be patient."

"I thought I heard horses some time back," Reilley said quietly.

"What do you mean?"

"Nothing. I thought I heard horses. Plenty of them."

"God!" Howell groaned. "That means the other soldiers are here, doesn't it? It means they'll be ready to kill us now."

"It means nothing," Chan Li put in. "All is speculation. We must try not to think of the worst."

Ki found her shoulder in the darkness and squeezed it. "I do not think they will do it in the darkness anyway. It would lose much of its effectiveness," he said dryly.

They heard a particularly loud snapping from above. A shower of chips rained down.

"That did it," Verdugo said. "They'll have heard that one."

"They're all half drunk by now," Joe Dawes said. "Didn't you see them, drinking tequila all day."

"They still got ears, don't they?"

"Someone's coming," said Ben the elephant trainer, in a taut whisper.

Ki glanced toward the ceiling, saw Quayle freeze, and moved back against the wall himself, poised and relaxed. The door banged open and Ki thought at first that Verdugo was right—they had heard the noises Quayle was making.

There were only three guards visible—Hector and two other Mexicans, one of them the man with the huge gut. Hector entered, the other two holding back, their bodies silhouetted starkly against the rectangle of sundown sky visible through the open door.

"You, Señorita, come with me," Hector said to Jessie, smiling lazily, gloatingly.

"What for?" she asked.

Ki had started to move forward. Hector's rifle found him and remained trained on his stomach. "Back up, tall man," Hector warned. "The lady is going with us."

"For what purpose?"

153

"I don't know," Hector said. "I can't even guess." His voice changed and grew menacing. "Chato Cruz wants her, that's all. He's going to have her. You understand that, *cabrón?* Don't you move forward again. I know you are a fancy fighter. But not so fast as this bullet, eh?"

There was nothing Ki could do, nothing at all. Shame and anger burned through his bowels as he watched Jessie taken by the arm toward the door. He risked a glance at Quayle. The Ranger was ready to leap, poised and set, but Ki shook his head.

As if to himself he said, "There's nothing we can do just now."

Hector glanced back at him, frowning slightly. "There is nothing you can do, ever again," he said. Then they went out, the closing of the door cutting out the purple rectangle of light.

"Get that opening broken out," Ki said, hissing through his teeth. He didn't have to urge Quayle on. The Ranger was working frantically now, not concerned with silence, but only with freedom. He had to get out of there, had to. Cruz had Jessie, and he wasn't a man to play nicely.

Chato Cruz liked his women spunky. He liked them frightened or angry or plain mean. All of these suited him much more than the acquiescent ones or those who tried to pretend they really cared for him, who lay there soft and yielding.

This one would not be like that. And what a beauty— *Madre de Dios!* He couldn't wait to get that shirt off her back and lift that skirt high up over her head. He stood in the doorway, watching, smoking a thin cigar. He glanced toward the headquarters building, as the European called it, but there was no sign of Waldo or of Cheney. That was good; Chato wanted no interference.

He turned and walked into his private cabin, picking up the tequila bottle from the table.

154

"It is time," he decided abruptly. The thought wasn't new, but the determination was. "It is time to eliminate that weakling Cheney. It is time to kill the European. I have no need for them."

He was silent. He realized that he had been talking to the walls, speaking aloud, and that troubled him a little. He pushed out his lower lip thoughtfully and took another deep drink.

He could hear footsteps now, and he grinned, finishing his drink, feeling the slow swelling begin in his groin. *Ai,* such a woman!

"Chato?"

Cruz's eyes narrowed, and Hector cursed silently. He had forgotten again. He corrected himself.

"General Cruz. I have brought the prisoner."

"Very good."

And he had brought her. There was fire in the girl's eyes. Her long copper-blond hair fell down across her shoulders and back.

"Go away," he told Hector, and Hector remembered to sketch a salute before he went out, closing the door behind him.

And Jessie Starbuck stood there staring at the dark and dangerous Chato Cruz, watching as he slowly poured another drink, wondering frantically how she could get out of here. She knew a few tricks of her own, tricks Ki had taught her, but Cruz was a cautious and animal-clever man.

"Welcome," he said softly, "to my headquarters. I am going to have you, woman. If there was any doubt in your mind, that is what I brought you here for."

And Jessie felt her breath catch as he started toward her. There was no way out. The door behind her was undoubtedly guarded. There was only a single low window, and to get to it she would have to get past Chato.

Chato came on, slowly unbuttoning his shirt, revealing

155

a scarred torso, an Indian bead necklace.

"I am going to have you," Cruz repeated, and with loathing Jessie surrendered to the idea; that was exactly what was going to happen.

"Hurry."

"I can't go any faster." Quayle ripped another section of board loose. He had a gap twelve to fourteen inches high between wall and roof now. "I'm going out. Which one's his cabin?"

"I don't know," Ki said. He leaped up and started toward Quayle. "I must go as well."

"It's the one on the end. The north end," Reilley said. "I saw Cruz go into that cabin."

"All right. Goodbye. Luck." Then Quayle forced his body into the gap he had made. His head and then his arm, and then his left leg, the rough, splintered boards scratching at his back, chest, and legs.

"Wait a minute," Ki hissed, but Quayle wasn't waiting for anyone.

"I'm going. Don't try to stop me, Ki."

Ki wasn't exactly doing that. He was into the rafters now, watching the Ranger force his body into the gap and through it, with a tearing of fabric, to disappear into the outside darkness.

Quayle hung by his fingertips for a brief moment, looking to the right and then to the left. He saw one man far away in the trees, but he wasn't looking his way Quayle moved off through the shadows, running in a crouch.

He glanced back and saw Ki behind him. Ki, taller yet, had a hell of a time squeezing through. He hit the ground hard, then rose, dusting his hands off, and turned to meet the buttplate of a Winchester rifle.

It rang off Ki's skull and he went down to stay down, the dust lifting beneath his nostrils.

"Take him back in?" the guard asked.

"No," Carlos answered. "The European wants him now. He wants to kıll him now. Tie him up. Hand and foot. Watch this side of the stockage. Send someone in to count heads. More may have escaped."

Ki thought he heard voices, thought he felt rough hands on him, turning him this way and that, but he wasn't sure. The sea of fire that surged through his mind made hearing and thinking very difficult. *Jessie*. There was something the matter with Jessie. She needed help! What the trouble was, he did not know exactly. He tried to shake his head and clear it, but it was no use. He just knew he had to rise, he had to find her, but when he tried, they clubbed him down again and the sea of fire became a black, black ocean that swallowed up consciousness.

Quayle was still running, swiftly, softly. He saw the shadowy figure in front of him too late, and he knew he couldn't avoid the guard. He didn't try. Quayle barreled on into him, hammering down with his fist, and the Mexican's head spun around with a satisfying crack. He went down in a heap with Quayle on top of him, holding a hand over the outlaw's mouth in case he should cry out.

But he wasn't going to be crying out for a long while. He was out cold. Quayle ripped the rifle from his hands, tore off his bandolier of ammunition, and raced on, cutting between two buildings, the headquarters building and some sort of barn where green hay, imported from somewhere, filled the night air with its peculiar scent.

There was a lighted window ahead of Qyayle now, and he heard voices. He paused, pressing himself to the wall of the building. His chest rose and fell heavily. He had hastily slipped the bandolier over one shoulder, and he stood gripping the rifle with two hands.

He wiped the sweat from his eyes with the back of his hand. He heard the voices again and started on frantically.

157

One of the voices was a woman's, and there was only one woman it could be.

He was beneath the window now, crouched low. Glass crashed within the cabin, and Chato Cruz laughed.

"Go ahead, tear the place apart! I like you, woman. Ow! That one hurt! Come here, wildcat!"

Quayle sucked in a shallow breath and lifted up. He saw Jessie trying to tear free of Chato's grasp, saw her eyes widen as she spotted Quayle.

Cruz was all over her, pawing, slapping, grabbing. His mind was on his crotch and not on security. Quayle was over the window ledge and to Cruz in one long stride. The barrel of the Winchester went up and descended sharply.

Chato Cruz slumped to the floor, his lip curled back, one unseeing eye staring up at Quayle.

"John . . ."

"Come on. Quickly."

"Ki . . ."

Quayle shook his head. He didn't know what had happened to Ki. He thought that Ki had followed him out of the stockade, and that by now the others would have gotten out too, but if that was so, some of them would have been spotted and there would have been shouting and gunfire.

"We can't worry about him just now. He can take care of himself."

Jessie knew Quayle was right, but it went against her grain not to worry about him. She bent and picked up Chato Cruz's pistol and gunbelt, then nodded.

"Let's go."

Quayle glanced toward the door, expecting company at any second, but then the guards must have had orders not to come in for any reason. He went to the window. Looking out, he saw nothing but a dull, rising moon out on the flats beyond the mesa. Quayle stepped over the windowsill and into the night.

He paused, crouching, looking left and then right.

"Hurry," he whispered, helping Jessie over the sill.

"Which way?" she asked, but he could only shake his head. There was no activity outside, which could either mean that the escape had gone very well, or that it had floundered badly.

Ki should have been there by now, if he had gotten away. Quayle whispered into Jessie's ear, "Let's find a place where we can see the stockade."

She agreed instantly. It was that or run for the trees beyond the camp, and they wouldn't last long there. Nor would she leave Ki behind.

They walked behind the windowless barn and to the shadows of the trees beyond, where they stood staring at the stockade. Nothing seemed to move. Then Jessie saw the guard walking his post behind the building, and she tugged sharply on Quayle's sleeve.

He fell back and let his eyes follow her jabbing finger. Simultaneously they both saw the shadowy figure lying on the ground. Both of them knew it was Ki, even in the darkness.

Quayle started slowly forward, Jessie beside him, but at that moment three more men rounded the corner of the stockade, all of them armed, moving cautiously. Jessie and the Ranger moved farther back into the darkness of the trees and stood watching, feeling helpless as Ki was pulled upright and lugged off.

"We've got to—" Jessie began, but halted abruptly. What *could* they do?

They saw torchlight against the sky then, across the compound near the other barracks. Ki was being taken that way, and as Jessie and Quaywe followed, they saw that the torches were being used to illuminate a cleared circle. A ring of combat.

The new soldiers never came, Jessie said to herself, as

159

if that fact could make the fight impossible. Waldo had decided not to wait, apparently.

Quayle grabbed Jessie's arm and drew her back against the wall of what appeared to be a cookshack. Three slow-walking, chattering Mexicans walked past, an arm's length away from where they stood pressed to the shadows.

Jessie and Quayle circled around the firelit area, coming up from the west again. Quayle looked up to the roof of the unused barracks and nodded to Jessie. He tossed the rifle up on the roof and boosted her up. Then he jumped, grabbed the eaves, and swung up. They bellied forward to lie looking down at the scene below.

Ki, propped up between two men, his feet and hands still bound, stood woozily staring across the clearing. The big man stood there, watching back. Waldo. The Death Angel.

He had his shirt off now, and he might have been hewn of oak. Muscles bulged and rippled with every slight movement, even with the taking of breath. That face, which had appeared dull and innocent, now seemed fierce and malevolent. He was a killing thing, waiting to get to his task.

Jessie glanced at John, who was hunkered down behind his rifle, a rifle that was virtually useless. He could kill the Death Angel, but it wouldn't save Ki's life in the end. And Chato would have Jessie back.

Chato . . . he was walking unsteadily toward the firelit ring. Jessie picked him out of the group of shorter men around him. She also saw Ray Cheney, looking irritated, as if he couldn't understand what this had to do with making him emperor of the new land.

"His hands and feet," Jessie whispered. Ki's circulation would have been cut off by the bonds. He was also dizzy from the blow on the head; that was obvious even from their distance. Waldo knew it. He had to. And he was going

160

to take advantage of it, apparently. Fair play didn't enter into his thinking.

He was going to kill Ki, that was the assignment. It would be done.

The circus people, tied together with a long rope, were being led out of the stockade. They would all have the chance to watch it. Jessie saw Chan Li, her head high, her movements unsteady as she came forward to watch her man executed.

"John . . ." Jessie gripped the Ranger's sleeve. He shook his head, just shook his head. There was nothing they could do to save the man below. He was going to die, and there was just nothing anyone could do about it.

★

Chapter 16

Jessie watched with frozen horror as the Mexicans unbound Ki's hands and feet. He was half-led into the center of the firelit ring where he was to face the Death Angel, the man whose life *was* killing.

Ki knew what was happening. He wasn't unaware of the situation, the firelight, the bulk of Waldo, the dark, amused eyes encircling him. It wasn't his mind that was unalert, but his body. There was a tingling in his fingertips that did not bode well. His feet were heavy, stonelike. His eyes refused to focus properly. A numbness in his left side affected that shoulder and arm.

Waldo was there, huge, implacable, his bulk blotting out the light behind him.

"Ki. You must die. You are an enemy of the revolution. Do you deny the charge?" Waldo still insisted on his quasi-legal jargon. Ki smiled thinly.

"I do not deny that I oppose you."

"Then you oppose the revolution."

"Revolution?" Ki's mind turned slowly. "A revolution is an act born of the dissatisfaction of the governed with their government. None of you are citizens of the United States, which owns this territory. It is therefore not revolution." He knew that the arguments were pointless now, but he was playing for time. His hands were starting to tingle with life now, as the blood rushed back into them. His vision was clearing a little. "This is common theft, Waldo, or whatever your real name is."

"No." Waldo smiled. "There is nothing common about a million square miles, my Japanese adversary."

"The thought is common. Taking through force. With no ideal behind your action but your own power and glory."

Ki's feet were coming to life now. He continued to watch Waldo, who so badly wanted to make a show of this that he was perhaps letting his advantage slip away.

Only perhaps. For they said that the Death Angel was indomitable, and perhaps he was. Ki saw no doubt at all in the big man's eyes; and the thought came to him suddenly that Waldo knew exactly what was happening, that Ki's nerves and muscles were coming back to life, that he was toying with him.

"Then there is nothing you wish to say? No farewells to make?" Waldo asked, his voice almost soft.

"None. And you?"

Waldo smiled then, bowed, and took two steps backward. Ki watched him, and as he did so he tried to still his mind, to use force of will to reach into the depths of his being, to find the last reserves. He was not defeated until it had been done—but even if he did defeat Waldo, could he survive? Chato Cruz was there, and Chato's way was simpler—a trigger would be pulled and Ki would go down.

There is no time to think beyond the battle, Ki thought. *Only concentrate on the man. Concentrate and assimilate.*

163

It would be necessary to solve the Death Angel's style quickly. That was the key to victory. Would he use an inside or outside attack? Were his feet his favored weapons? *No, the hands,* Ki thought. *With a man that size, always the hands.*

Ki bowed also and waited, his hands coming up, his arms weaving sinuously before him, as Waldo watched. The big man nodded as if with secret satisfaction and came in. The firelit night had gone silent. The men in the watching circle seemed to be holding their breath collectively.

Waldo yelled fiercely, gathering his strength, putting his explosive force in focus. He leaped, his leg coming in for a straight kick at Ki's throat. Ki blocked the strike with a forearm and was spun halfway around by the force of the kick. As he had known all along, Waldo had the power of a mule in his legs, yet he possessed the sort of skill a dumb brute never learned.

Ki struck back, aiming his kick at the kneecap. The Death Angel blocked the kick with his left foot and centered a *nakadata-ippon-ken* knuckle strike on the nerve bundle in Ki's left shoulder. Ki yelled with pain and anger and stepped back. The Death Angel, suddenly overconfident, tried to follow up with a spinning kick, but Ki chopped the side of his right hand savagely against the column of muscle on Waldo's neck, momentarily stunning him.

Crouching, his hands out flat, Ki executed a *yonhon-nukite-uchi,* or spear-hand thrust at Waldo's solar plexus, but the big man avoided it, turning to come in with a heel kick aimed at Ki's chin.

Ki ducked and whirled, moving fluidly now, all of his earlier wooziness overpowered by the need to survive, bolstered by years of training. But each time he accelerated his pace, using tricks he had not needed for years against lesser opponents, the Death Angel accelerated his own defenses, his own bludgeoning attack.

The side of Waldo's hand, like a cleaver, slammed into Ki's unprotected neck as he underestimated the speed of the strongman and paid the price for his error: stunning, gut-tightening pain. Earlier, Waldo had been smiling, but now he had lost that smile. There was nothing amusing about death; Waldo knew he had found an adversary worthy of his talents, and it was going to take his full skill to execute Ki.

Good. He did not like to take fools who knew nothing and twist their heads off. There was no pleasure in that. What sort of pride could a man take in such work?

Ki tried for the groin with a left-footed kick, and the Death Angel crossed his hands before him, blocking it, trying to take Ki's ankle and overbalance him, but Ki spun away, using his free foot to strike Waldo's hands and break the grip.

Ki missed a *tobi-geri*, a leaping kick, as Waldo shifted his body just slightly to one side, like a matador dodging a fast and deadly bull. Ki hit the ground hard and rolled away automatically, before Waldo's stamping heel could crush his throat.

He rolled and came up, but didn't find his balance quickly enough. Waldo's foot met his ribcage, and only a last-second lunge away from the blow saved Ki from a shattering of bone, splinters driven into vital organs.

Waldo came in more confidently now. Ki shook his head and came up in a defensive spin. He had not underestimated his foe; he had overestimated his own body's readiness to fight. Still he was slowed and confused by the blow to the head. Still his arms and legs were leaden.

And Waldo knew it!

Damn him, he had known. He had been pretending to give Ki time, perhaps to trick his own savage ego into believing the combatants were on even ground. Ki ducked a high kick and his crossed hands fended off a side-hand blow, but he was being driven back inexorably, the blows of the Death Angel landing more frequently, hammering his body, and he was unable to set himself, unable to use his superior speed to duck away.

The roar of the crowd swelled suddenly against his ears. He could hear them cheering in two languages. He could see Cruz, darkly amused, and Cheney, excited and mesmerized. And he could see Chan Li, small, angry, and afraid.

The Death Angel landed a solid blow to the liver, which Ki was barely able to deflect with a downward block, a *gedan-barai*. Ki was taken down by a back-kick, but he rolled away again and was pursued by the plodding Death Angel. He tried to rise and was met by a two-handed blow to the chest. His heart screamed a protest from deep within his chest, and Ki went down again.

"Jessie . . ."

John Quayle tried to grab her arm, but he was too slow. Watching the battle until she could watch it no more, Jessie had come to a long shot of an idea. It wasn't much, but it beat hell out of seeing Ki slowly smashed to death by a sadistic giant.

John grabbed for her arm but missed, and Jessie slid down the roof of the empty barracks. She dropped silently to the ground as a roar of blood-sport pleasure reached her from the crowd beyond the building.

Quayle landed softly beside her.

"What are you going to do?"

"Follow me."

She started off toward the trees and the circus wagons that lay beyond, out of the glare of the firelight. Another savage cheer went up from behind them, but Jessie didn't allow herself to look back.

The sleepy guard appeared suddenly before them. Opening his mouth to speak, he found Jessie's derringer shoved into his face. His mouth shut abruptly.

Quayle tapped him behind the ear with his stolen rifle and they moved on, stepping over the guard's body.

"What are you going to do?" Quayle asked, clutching at her sleeve.

"Save Ki."

It wasn't much of an answer. There wasn't much substance to her words. The emotion was there, however, the need to save Ki. She would do it if she had to go into the firelit circle and throw herself on the Death Angel. Quayle understood that. He questioned her no more.

Jessie opened the door to her own wagon, entered quickly, took down a lamp from the wall and scooped a bundle of matches from a drawer, and went out again. Running to the empty lion cage, she pulled the burner from the lamp and poured the oil from the lamp's well on the floor of the cage, spreading it over the dry wood and straw as best she could. Then she struck one of the matches and threw it on the dark stain of lamp oil. It ignited with a soft *whoosh!* and a flaring of yellow light, and within a few seconds the tinder-dry planking of the cage was engulfed in crackling flames.

Quayle grabbed Jessie's arm and took off at a run around the darkened barracks and back toward the ring. As they ran, they caught occasional glimpses of men running toward the fire, shouting.

As they took cover in the shadow of the barracks, they could see the Death Angel hovering over Ki's recumbent form. But then, as Jessie watched with stunned amazement, Ki got to his feet and attacked, a windmilling, spinning tornado of fury. Waldo fell back momentarily in confusion.

How it had happened, Ki couldn't have said. He only knew as he lay on the ground for the third time that he was beaten. Beaten! He would not allow it. It could not be. Deep

167

within himself was a small, pulsing thing, a kernel of strength that was his being, that throbbed and cried out to him. Ki rested. It was not for a long while, only a fraction of a second. A brief moment during which every muscle, every fiber relaxed and he looked deep within himself, feeling the life force, the root of his knowledge and skills.

And then he came to his feet, and Waldo, striking out, found his blow blocked, felt the counterthrust, the pain in the hollow of his stomach, the searing white heat in the nerves in his neck as Ki's solid blow struck home. Ki struck again as Waldo fell back, looking around in confusion.

Waldo was aware of a fire behind him, of Cruz's people running off to investigate, but he was only peripherally aware of these things. His attention was focused on the dervish before him, the whirling, spinning Japanese who thrust with a stiffened hand, side-kicked, kneed the groin, ducked under a counterblow, came up with a strike at Waldo's throat and then an elbow to the plexus. Waldo backed away in near panic. Then he tripped. His heel hit a rock and down he went. An involuntary cheer went up from the watching circus people and Ki turned toward them, realizing that the combat would have to be postponed. Now was the time to make an escape, to get the circus folks free.

There were three guards watching still, who, seeing the new intent on Ki's face, backed away, lifting their rifles, watching each other warily.

The circus people had begun to walk forward as well, Reilley and Verdugo in the lead.

"Stay back," one of the guards said coldly. He cocked his weapon, the sound clearly audible, menacing in the night.

"Why don't you just drop that?" the man in the shadows behind him said.

It was Quayle, and Jessie was with him. The guard hesitated only a moment, then dropped his rifle, as did the others. Behind Ki, Waldo was groaning, getting heavily to hands and knees, the firelight streaking his face with moving shadows.

"Come on. Now!" Jessie urged them all. "That fire won't divert them for long."

She was right. Ki picked up one of the rifles and tossed the others to Verdugo and Reilley, and they started running, running into the night.

They heard the guard call after them. "Run hard. Run as long as you like. You ain't gettin' anywhere anyway, you damned fools."

The bastard was right. Where were they going to go, isolated as they were, surrounded by gunmen? Nevertheless, none of them would have chosen to remain, to stand and be slaughtered without a chance to fight back.

Ki was leading the way now. He climbed a low sandstone dome west of the camp and stopped for breath and to count heads. Some of the circus people were lagging badly. They weren't all athletes like Quayle.

"You beat him badly," Chan Li said. She was beside Ki in the darkness, her soft eyes glowing in the starlight as she looked up to him. "You defeated him. Now he must go away in shame."

"It's not that way with him. It's a combat to the death. He must come again and again, until one of us is dead. And if he can't defeat me honorably, then he must murder me."

There was no answer to that, and Chan Li didn't try to utter one. She stood by him silently, waiting for everyone to gather.

They stood together, determined but overmatched by far. They could see activity down below, and plenty of it. Some people were saddling their horses, but others didn't seem to be worried about it. The prisoners weren't going far.

"Cruz will be in charge now," Ki guessed.

"Not Cheney?"

"Cheney's done his work. He brought the money and the weapons in. He's expendable."

"Shouldn't we make a run for it?" asked Howell.

"Do you think so?" Quayle said coldly.

Jessie was a little kinder. "There's just nowhere to go, Mr. Howell."

"We can't . . . are we just going to wait for them to kill us?"

"For the man who brought us here, you're pretty worried all of a sudden," Reilley said.

"I'm sorry," Howell said, and he sounded genuinely sorry. "I just want to know what's going to happen now."

"Now," Ki said softly, *"we're* going to attack *them*."

There was an incredible silence following those words. People looked at each other in the darkness. They couldn't believe they had heard properly.

"Do you mean it?" Joe Dawes asked.

"Yes."

"We're not all warriors like you," said Ben, the elephant trainer.

"I understand that. But what else is there to do? We have no food or water. Are we to hide out here for a few hours until daylight comes? Then they will kill us. Should we run? Then they will ride us down. There is no other option but to fight."

"God," someone moaned in near despair.

Quayle spoke up. "He's right. I don't like it, but he is right. There's just no option."

"What have we got? Three rifles."

Schupe, who was holding up surprisingly well, said, "There's other weapons in my wagon. They took all the captured guns and threw them in there."

170

"And your wagon, Ki."

"But the wagons are being watched."

"There won't be much of a guard. They won't be expecting us to come back. Anyway, we need more weapons," Ki said.

Howell was near tears. "Sure. And then what do we have? Two dozen circus performers and roustabouts against an army of well-armed, well-trained men."

"I did not create the situation," Ki said quietly. "I'm only trying to find the best way of dealing with it. I have no better idea. Have you?"

There was no answer, of course. There was no other way. The fire near the wagons had burned down now. The scent of ash was heavy in the air as Ki, Quayle, Jessie, and Reilley moved through the darkness. The others were just over the low ridge behind the circus wagons. There was no point in all of them trying this approach. The people accompanying Ki were the ones he trusted. Except for Chan Li. Was it protectiveness that had caused him to leave her behind? His reasoning had been that he needed a cool head to keep watch over the others. Maybe. He only knew he cared for her.

The soldiers of Chato Cruz were beginning to fan out and search for the escaped prisoners, but not enthusiastically, not thoroughly. Morning would be soon enough for them, when they could see, when the tequila had worn off. The prisoners were going nowhere; everyone knew that. What they didn't expect was to be attacked. They were easy pickings.

Ki took out one man with an *atemi* hold from behind. He didn't even make a sound. When, a few minutes later, Quayle had to knock a man out, it was equally simple. The man was already half asleep.

Ki looked at Jessie and she nodded. They were at the

perimeter of the wagon circle now, moving toward his wagon, smelling dead fire, feeling the heat of it, hearing the hissing and growling of the big cats, still caged, hungry, mean.

There was no problem finding the wagon, no problem entering. Ki filled his vest pockets with *shuriken*, wrapped a *surushin* around his waist, and, after only a moment's hesitation, moved to the crate of dynamite in the corner and lifted several bundles, stuffing caps and lengths of fuse into his pockets.

"Ready?"

It was Quayle at the doorway, arms filled with the stolen weapons. Ki nodded and looked around, wondering if he had forgotten something vital, then went out into the night, dropping to the ground to find Jessie and Reilley ready to go, their arms, like Quayle's, loaded with weapons wrapped in blankets to keep metal from clicking against metal as they made their hasty, silent retreat toward the ridge.

Their army was there waiting. Few, frightened, unwilling. If there had ever been a more uneven battle, Ki could not imagine it.

To the east, the blood-red sun was rising.

★

Chapter 17

The fiery sun rose, and its light washed out the torches below. They could see Cruz's men like dark insects crawling across the land. Some of them were mounted, riding in gradually widening circles across the broken mesa top. A party of a dozen or so had gone out earlier, down the trail to the desert flats. Others walked singly or in pairs or groups along the arroyos, through the brushy hills.

Ki watched them with intense concentration. Jessie was on one side of him, Quayle on the other. They held a whispered battle conference.

"What do we do? Stay in one group?"

"We could split our force. They'd never storm ther way up that slope. Look at the brush."

"They could burn it. And us. Besides, we won't last a day without water. They can sit there and wait if they choose to."

"Then what?" Quayle's face was lined with worry, streaked with dirt.

"We attack," Ki said, "as I told you before. We must attack Cruz's force."

"Ki, be reasonable!" Jessie said.

"I am being reasonable. It is the only chance. To lie here and wait to die is certainly slower, but it offers no chance for survival." Ki had been counting heads as he talked, seeing that Cruz's vaunted army numbered no more than forty men. Subtract the dozen who had ridden out earlier, and there were a nearly manageable number. Where the expected reinforcement army from the south had gone, Ki had no idea. He only hoped to God they lost their way.

"Well?" Jessie asked Quayle.

"Ki's the general," Quayle said, although he too was a soldier. His wars had been different, however—a few border thieves, a handful of outlaws, Comanches raiding settlers. These were fought in ways Quayle understood. This was beyond him. Ki's life was struggle. If anyone could direct this combat, it was Ki.

And Ki had ideas. They sounded slightly mad to Quayle, but maybe they needed a mad plan to survive this day.

"Jessie," Ki said, "I want you to stay beside me."

"All right." She looked at Quayle and shrugged slightly. "You know, Ki, the way things look right now—"

"I know, Jessie, but don't think of it. We will make it. I feel it. Now—get me Verdugo and Ben. And Chan Li." Jessie slid down off the ridge, and Ki told Quayle, "Take your force around to the east and attack from the trees. Keep up a constant fire."

"Some of my people can't hit a thing."

"The distraction is what's important, John. You have Dawes and Reilley. You have Colonel Payne. That old man can shoot."

"All right. Ki—good luck."

They shook hands briefly and then Quayle was gone,

174

leading his ragged army away. Tumblers, a sharpshooter, a sword-swallower, a clown or two, roustabouts. Ki shook his head, suffering a few doubts himself.

"I hope I have not led you all to disaster," he said, but he didn't dwell on it. He was doing all he could.

Ki's own small unit was prepared to move out. Chan Li, Verdugo, and Ben.

"This is it?" the elephant trainer asked.

"This is it." Ki smiled. "It is all we have." He squatted to cut fuse and prepare his dynamite. Verdugo's eyes opened a little wider at the sight of it.

"What the hell would a man carry something like that around for?"

"One never knows what may become necessary," Ki said, glancng up. "We must use whatever is at hand. Chan Li—you know exactly what to do?"

"Yes, Ki."

"Fine. Verdugo?"

"I think so. Seems a little dangerous."

"It is. Did you think today would not be dangerous?"

Verdugo smiled faintly, shaking his head.

"You stick with me," Ben said. "I won't let you down."

Ki gave Jessie three bundles of dynamite, four sticks in each. She already had a rifle and her belt gun. Now Ki added to that arsenal a half-dozen throwing stars.

"She know what to do with those?" Verdugo asked.

"I assure you she does," Ki said.

"Good. That's what I need. Assurance, and plenty of it," the animal trainer said quite seriously.

Ki looked again at Jessie and nodded. The smiles they exchanged privately were far from reassuring. But there was no other way.

They moved off through the brushy ravine, watching the sun rise, the shadows shorten. There was no one at the circus camp. Nothing stirred but the raging big cats, the hungry horses, the placid elephants.

"Poor bastards," Verdugo said with genuine concern as he walked from cage to cage, looking at his cats. His face was still battered from trying to protect his lion, and Ki knew the man would take another beating to protect the tiger or the panther. Verdugo was at the leopard's cage, saying something in secret to his charge.

"It will be all right?" Ki asked.

"Yes."

"Ben?"

"I won't have any problem. Are we ready?"

"When Chan Li is."

The Chinese woman had reappeared from her wagon's interior, carrying her robed arms folded. She was ready. Ki asked her, "Have you all you will need?"

"Let us hope so."

Ki smiled. "Yes. Let us hope so."

The firing began from across the flats. Quayle's army had opened up. A scream of pain drifted to them. At least one outlaw had paid the price.

"Now!" Ki said. "It is time."

They came out of the trees with Verdugo leading the way. There was a single outlaw blocking their path. The first thing the Mexican saw of Verdugo's small, very special guerrilla force was the flash of tawny flank, a curled-back lip revealing savage white fangs. Then he felt the sudden crushing impact as the panther hit him. The *bandido* went down screaming as the big cat mauled him.

Chato Cruz was holed up in the headquarters building, staring out with bleary eyes, trying to figure out what was happening. Attacking? The crazy circus people, attacking his soldiers?

Gunfire from behind took down three men before his

eyes. One was Carlos, who lay pawing at the earth, trying to drag himself forward on a shattered leg.

Cruz looked to his right and saw only one old man, dressed in buckskins. The man lifted his rifle to his shoulder and fired five times. Five hits!

Chato fired back wildly, but Colonel Payne was out of pistol range, and the sharpshooter calmly continued to fire. Chato Cruz bellowed a curse. His men were at the headquarters building now, clattering and rattling around as they tried to decide what to do. They hadn't expected anything like this. Chato had to scream at them.

"Get to the windows. Get to the windows!"

"We must attack!" This was Ray Cheney, come from out of the shadows, wearing the red uniform he had had made in El Paso for his role as El Presidente. "Get up, you men. I am in charge here, not Cruz. We will attack on the count of three. One—"

Chato Cruz shot him through the heart.

Cheney folded up and fell, bleeding his life out onto the wooden floor of a ramshackle building deep in New Mexico Territory, dying a would-be dictator's death.

Cruz went back to the window. He saw an incredible sight near the old barracks. A man ran toward him, hands raised. His shirt was ripped from his body, and blood smeared his face. The tiger hit him from behind, paws over the shoulders, dragging him down, tearing at him with fangs and claws. Someone shot at the tiger but missed, and they saw the animal break off its attack as if recalled by someone behind the barracks.

"Who's left out there?" Cruz demanded. The firing from the trees was fierce, constant. Bullets whined off the walls of the building. A man at the other window was hit in the throat, hurled back by the bullet to lie strangling on the floor.

"Hector has his people behind the new barracks. Ten men, Chato uh, General Cruz."

Cruz was too enraged to notice the breach of his new etiquette. His eyes narrowed, searching for Hector and his men. Yes, they were firing back, and now the idiot was finally going to do what he should have done earlier—send half of his force to flank the circus people in the woods. That old sharpshooter was good, but he couldn't hit them all.

Chato saw the soldiers make their move, rushing across the open space. Then he saw the white horse. Someone was clinging to it, riding low, behind the horse. There was a burst of something like a bomb, only quieter, and then a vast red cloud drifted across the clearing and Chato could see nothing.

"What the hell's that!"

Anyone who had ever seen one of Chan Li's shows could have told him. The smoke bombs she usually flung from her sleeves caused brief, harmless explosions. This time she had used many of them, and the red smoke concealed everything while the reinforcements moved up to attack Chato's headquarters.

That was what Chato could not accept, and that was what defeated him: they were *attacking*.

At first sight of the reinforcements, one of Cruz's hard men screamed in terror. Cruz's own eyes opened wide. They emerged from the red smoke, gargantuan, their trunks lifted, trumpeting. The elephants were charging directly at the headquarters building, and on their backs were the crazy Japanese, the elephant man, and that copper-haired hellcat.

It was like a nightmare of war. Chato Cruz was not an educated man, and he didn't know of the centuries of history when the great beasts were commonly used to make war, to crush the enemy's will and, if necessary, his flesh and bones.

Horses ran before the trumpeting elephants in blind panic. Cruz fired twice, missed apparently, and heard his pistol's hammer fall on an empty chamber. The Japanese had something in his hand, something he hurled at the old barracks where Hector was pinned down.

"Madre de Dios!" Cruz figured it out instantly. He had seen dynamite before, and he hit the floor as the bundle Ki had thrown went up.

The force of the explosion shook the building. A wave of heat washed over them. One of Chato's men was struck by a flying timber. There was a second explosion, nearly as powerful, and then, as Cruz lay cowering, the terrible knowledge came to him of what was happening, as the first elephant simply walked into the jerry-built headquarters building and the walls collapsed.

Cruz saw the timber overhead falling, saw the great foot descending, and there was just time to scream out an enraged, almost childish scream, which was cut off short by the crushing weight on his chest.

Jessie Starbuck was standing in the middle of the clearing as the smoke drifted away. Ben had led his animals off. Verdugo was rounding up his tiger. The dead were everywhere. It was incredible, impossible, but the circus people had suffered no casualties. Joe Dawes had been hit by a branch cut from the tree he was sheltered under, but that was all. They stood together, smudged and exhausted, a weary, triumphant army.

Jessie didn't let them get settled or complacent.

"We've got to move now. Get your wagons hitched."

"But why?"

"There are more of Chato's men down on the flats. There's an *army* coming up from the south. We don't want to be taken again."

"She's right," John Quayle said. "We've got to move, and now."

179

"I can't go through anything like this again," one of the clowns cried.

"Let's get it moving and hope we don't have to. Keep your weapons near at hand."

Ki was back from inspecting the destroyed headquarters building. He looked drawn, disgusted with the carnage. He was a warrior, but he did not like killing. He considered it a waste of the universe's efforts.

"Well?" Quayle asked.

"Cheney and Cruz."

"Not Waldo?"

"No. He was gone, but where I do not know. I think we will meet again one day."

"They're coming!" The shout was from Reilley, on top of the only undamaged barracks. They saw his finger point toward the road that led up from the flats below to the mesa top. "Get your guns! The rest of Cruz's men are coming in."

They took up their positions and waited grimly. Minutes ticked slowly past. It was hot. Jessie had gnats swarming in front of her face.

They saw the dust and then the horsemen, and Quayle yelled, "Hold your fire!" as the party of Texas Rangers came forward.

The man in charge was named Slade. He had one eye and thin gray hair. Just now he also had a bullet wound in his thigh.

"Why, damn you," Quayle demanded, "where have you been, Slade?"

"Oh, just lollygaggin' along," the old man said dryly. "What the hell happened here? A circus blow up?"

"I'll tell you later—you won't believe it anyway." Quayle was calmer now. "But where have you been? God, we could have used you, Slade."

"Yes, I'll bet." The old man swung down, needing help because of his leg. "First off, we was hit by Comanches. Lost Tom Draco. Shot through the head. Second, we run into the damnedest thing you ever saw—an army of Mexicans and Indians! Coming' up from the south. Must've been three hundred of 'em. Comin' here?" he asked, and Quayle nodded.

"What happened to them?"

"John—this is Comanche country."

"The Indians..."

"They hit 'em hard. Damnedest army I ever saw—they didn't have hardly a rifle among 'em."

"The rifles were here," John Quayle explained.

"Well, they should've been *there*. Comanches tried a few sorties and found out they weren't drawin' any fire, and then they had 'em. Ran over 'em. There's a lot of celebrating' in the Comanche lodges today. Many scalps."

"They didn't try you again?"

"They *tried* it." Slade winked. "We got guns."

"There was a smaller party of bandits, near the mesa..."

"Yes, there was," Slade said. "They hit us too. That was gravy—first time all week we wasn't overmatched. Now," he grunted, "what do you say we pack up and get back to civilization, John? Back to Texas."

★

Chapter 18

"It is a lot more civilized here, isn't it?" Jessie asked.

John Quayle had a little trouble answering. He was lying naked on his back in the Plainview, Texas, hotel room, and astraddle him was Jessie, her reddish blond hair down, her green eyes sparkling, her body swaying gently from side to side, her inner muscles working as she moved against John's deeply embedded shaft.

"Civilized," he said, as she lifted herself high so that only the head of his erection was in her. She looked down into his face, seeing the deep pleasure there. Smiling, she settled again and leaned forward, kissing his lips as she swayed from side to side, her breasts grazing his chest, stimulating her erect pink nipples.

Ki's room was down the hall, and the last time Jessie had seen him, the hotel management was taking a zinc bathtub in past him. A bathtub and two towels. Jessie wondered vaguely how Chan Li and Ki were both going to fit in that rather small tub.

Quayle sat up, his arms going around Jessie as he searched for her breasts with his hungry lips. She could feel his pulsing inside her, his breath on her nipples, and she sighed, leaning back, reaching behind her to touch him where he entered her, feeling her own juices on his manhood.

Quayle began to trembled and she stroked his head, going down with him as he arched his back and plumbed her depths, as his loins emptied and he clung to her, kissing her hair, her ears, her lips.

"Much more civilized," he said.

After a long while Jessie said, "You know she's here. She's been here waiting for you."

"Dorothy?"

"Yes."

"I know it. But that won't work out. *We* could work out, Jessie." He pushed back her hair and kissed her finely arched eyebrow.

"No. You know we can't. I've got my work, you've got yours."

"But—"

She stilled the objection with a deep kiss.

"Give her a chance, John. Any woman that's willing to kill for you must love you."

"We'll see. You know, Jessie, if we...maybe I could go along with you and Ki. I'm not so helpless, you know."

"Not at all." Her green eyes smiled briefly and then appeared to go far away.

John Quayle laughed with embarrassment. "Well, damn me, there's someone else, isn't there? Someone very important."

"Yes," she said, and they didn't discuss it anymore. They simply lay together in the bed, a sheet flung loosely over them, enjoying the very civilized atmosphere of Plainview, Texas.

* * *

Ki was dozing, lying atop his bed, wearing only his loose black cotton trousers. Chan Li lay curled against him, a dark blue silk robe thrown around her, her lovely raven hair in an ebony cascade across Ki's chest. They had a hot bath and made love, then slept, and both of them were reluctant to awaken and start a new day that would see them parted, perhaps never to meet again, except in memory.

Now Chan Li's hand began to stir from its resting place on his shoulder, and it moved, feather-light, down across his chest and belly, and crept under the waistband of his trousers to fondle the talisman of his manhood.

He opened one eye and looked at her peacefully smiling face. "Again, woman? So soon?"

"Yes, please," she said.

He sighed deeply and shook his head. "Ah, the Chinese—sex-crazy, all of them." He started to turn toward her—

And the door smashed open, slamming back against the wall, its lock tearing out a piece of the doorjamb with a shriek of splintering wood. Chan Li rolled quickly aside, and Ki sat up in bed, just staring.

He must have walked a hundred miles. He had yellow-gray whiskers on his jowls, his clothes were rags. His eyes were fierce and red. There was mud on his trouser legs up to his thighs.

"Die," the Death Angel said, and his words were slurred and indistinct, as Waldo's had been. "You die now. I am the victor."

Waldo hurled himself across the room and Ki rolled aside. Chan Li was in the corner, her hands to her mouth, her eyes wide as the strongman came at Ki.

Everything was different now; that was what Waldo didn't understand. Ki was well fed, relaxed, rested, and alert. It was a different man Waldo faced than the one he had fought on the mesa.

184

"You think you beat me," Waldo said heavily, his fists hanging at his side. "I walked. I came to prove you cannot beat the Angel!"

And he came in again, leaping high into the air, his terrible howl filling the room as he tried to crush Ki. But Ki had seen the move before; he knew Waldo's style. He ducked and came up under Waldo in a turning, rolling motion, his hands finding the point of Waldo's attack, the heels of his feet, carrying the strongman's thrust on past his head.

Waldo screamed again. His own leap had carried him to the hotel room's window, and Ki's maneuver had caused him to lose control of his body. His strike became a suicidal leap. The window, blue-white in the early sunlight, was before him, and then it was not.

Waldo's body smashed through the glass; it was a leap into eternity. His yell lasted a moment longer, until he hit the street below and broke his huge bull-like neck.

Ki stood with Chan Li, looking out at the giant's inert body. There was a crowd gathering below, gawking, chattering. Glass lay around Waldo's body, glittering in the sun like silver-blue flower petals.

"He is dead," Chan Li said, resting her head on his shoulder.

Pounding footsteps and raised voices could now be heard in the hallway outside the room as the hotel management and the morbidly curious came running to see whatever carnage the room might have to offer.

Ki turned Chan Li away from the window as Jessie appeared in the doorway. When she saw Ki, a look of immense relief passed across her features.

"Ki! Thank God you're all right! What—?"

"The Death Angel," Ki said. "I've sent him home."